LOVE SOMEBODY LIKE YOU

TRINITY LAKES ROMANCE BOOK FIVE

CAROLYN MILLER

CHAPTER ONE

There were ways to make a good first impression, and ways to not. Lexi Franklin sighed as she picked herself up from the muddied ground outside Trinity Life Church. This was not how she had envisaged making her grand entrance to Trinity Lakes. Not that she had ever imagined anything grand. These days, slinking in from halfway across the world was more her style.

"Oh, Lexi!" Her mother helped her stand, wincing at the dark brown stains on Lexi's white jeans-clad knees. That made two of them. "Are you okay?"

Way to go, feeling like someone two decades younger than her twenty-eight years, as her mother handed her a wet wipe. "I'm fine." She summoned a tight smile for those strangers who had paused to watch the show. Stupid heels. Why had she thought wearing heels to church a good idea?

Maybe she could put it down to jet lag. Or gracefulness lag. Except she'd never owned much poise except when it came to the medical world. And after what happened three months ago? That probably couldn't be said of her either.

"Want to go home and get changed?" her mother asked.

And miss Dad's message? "I'm fine. Can we go inside, please?"

She followed her mother up the three wooden steps and inside the white building. A glory of stained glass soared at the front, clear panes on either side revealing the view down the hill to the lake beyond. For a girl from a beachside city in Australia, the picture postcard prettiness of Trinity Lakes, with its quaint main street, shops, and hill-draped lakes, was a breath of fresh air. Literally.

Her passage to a pew was delayed as her mother felt it necessary to stop and chat with several people along the way, introducing Lexi each time.

Names slid past her ears: Kennedys, Ladans, Anderssons, but she didn't have space to retain information as embarrassment at her less-than-styled appearance choked any ability to recall names. So she smiled, said hello, and with immense gratitude finally reached her seat. "Hey, Dad."

Her father looked up from his notes and wrapped an arm around her. "How's my girl?"

"Looking forward to your message."

Smile lines deepened. "It's so good to have you here."

"It's good to be here."

As soon as she'd stepped off the plane at the Tri-Cities Airport, she'd known the difference, and it had nothing to do with the US summer temperatures. There was an ease here, like she was coming home, even if she hadn't lived in Trinity Lakes for years. Of course, part of that might've had something to do with being here with her parents, even if their protectiveness sometimes felt like a three-sizes-too-big winter coat. But she didn't mind. Much. After being scared for so long, it was nice to finally believe she could maybe feel safe again.

The service began, and her focus sank into rituals she was long familiar with—music, announcements, her dad's message. His words weren't new—she'd heard him say similar things about gratitude over the dinner table these past two nights—and she let them drift over her. Thankfulness might be okay for some, but she wasn't ready to be thankful for everything. Not yet. She played with the light scarf at her throat. Her mother looked at her, brow furrowed.

Lexi lowered her hand and took a moment to let her gaze slide around the congregation. The people seemed friendly, a mix of ages, ethnicities, and appearances, with everything from city-sleek types to those who looked more like farmers. The church had a nice feel, much like the town with its cute antique-style lampposts, and quirky shops. Trinity Lakes seemed a little different to what she remembered, new businesses, housing developments, new landscaping on the town limits that now displayed the poplars and *Welcome to Trinity Lakes* sign to full advantage. Same, same, but different. Or maybe that was just her. Unsurprising, considering what had happened.

Another hymn was sung, during which the collection plate was passed around, then they were released to be a blessing to the world.

She swallowed—she used to feel that way, like she could be a blessing—and managed to fake smile her way out the door, nodding to people she'd met earlier whose names she could no longer recall.

"Ah, Lynette. So this is Alexandra, all grown up." The pastor held out his hand. "Theo Ladan. It's been a while. Last I saw you, you were just finishing high school."

"It has been a while." Lexi shook his hand, wondering how much her parents had told him. Probably everything.

"It's good to see you here." His eyes were kind.

Yep. He definitely knew. "Thanks."

She readjusted the scarf at her throat, something which seemed to catch his attention, but he said nothing, only offering a smile, before a young family demanded his attention.

Exhale. She followed her mother outside, grasping the thin

metal handrail as she made her way down the steps back to the cobblestoned path. Her foot wobbled, and she slowed her pace. For goodness sake. How did brides and people with actual high heels manage on this path? It was bad enough to still be wearing knee stains announcing her status as Clumsy Girl. She had no wish to confirm the label with a round two.

"Lexi?" Her mother beckoned her to where she stood with an aristocratic-looking elderly woman. "I'd like you to meet a friend of mine. This is Mrs. Olivia Darcy."

Lexi offered a smile that was fifty percent more genuine. "Good morning." How many more people would she have to meet? How soon could she leave?

The woman nodded, her brow creasing as her gaze trickled over Lexi's muddied ensemble, as if she couldn't understand why Lexi hadn't returned home and changed.

"Lexi had a little accident on the way into church." Mum felt the need to explain, patting her on the shoulder.

Great. How to make her awkwardness more obvious: make it seem some other kind of accident more appropriate for a five-year-old. Mum might as well say she'd soiled her pants and be done with it. Even if that was technically true.

"How are you finding your stay so far?" Mrs. Darcy finally asked.

"I've only been here a couple of days," Lexi said. "I spent the first getting over jet lag, and the second getting familiar with the Bible college and surrounds again."

"Again?"

"Lexi was here with us until ten years ago."

Lexi nodded. "College—university—courses are cheaper in Australia, so it made sense to study nursing there. Then, when I got a job as a graduate—"

"A targeted graduate," Lexi's mother said proudly. "When the best and brightest are selected for immediate placements. That's what targeted means, right?"

Lexi's smile stiffened as she nodded. Targeted had proved to be the word, all right.

As her mother and Mrs. Darcy fell into conversation, Lexi's glance drifted across the milling congregants, falling on a nearby young couple who fitted the farmer category she'd observed before. The young woman wore a faded flowery dress, scuffed cowboy boots, and a dark braid. Lexi's own ensemble of white jeans, purple silk shirt, and heels couldn't have been more different. The young farmer—actually, scratch that. The man's dark jeans, boots, and big silver buckle suggested he could be a cowboy. He appeared fit and strong with broad shoulders, muscled arms, and a trim waist. That was purely a professional opinion, of course. She swallowed. She wasn't looking. He obviously was taken.

Her gaze lifted to meet his, and her breath suspended. His dark eyes and curly hair reminded her of a young Orlando Bloom, his features possessing a magnetic quality. Too much magnetism. She snatched her gaze away. Time to get out of here.

"Lexi?" Her dad drew her attention. "I'll just be a few minutes, okay?"

She nodded. "I'll wait near the car."

"I think a few of the younger folk like to eat at Joe's Diner." He pointed to a store on the corner near the park. "They're used to visitors joining them. You'd be very welcome, I'm sure."

"Thanks, but maybe another time."

He studied her for a moment, disappointment palpable in his dimmed smile and eyes. "It'll be a long summer without friends," he said.

"I'll make friends." And she would. Just not today. Not when there was still so much to process.

She flipped her long mane of strawberry blonde hair over her shoulder and pivoted on the path, but her movement was too fast, and her stupid heel wobbled, then snapped off, and she was falling, falling—

———

Oof!

Jackson Reilly swung an arm down and collected the visitor, saving her just before she hit the deck. His grip tightened as he stared into eyes the color of summer hills, the pale green holding something that looked a lot like fear.

"Gotcha."

She shivered, then wriggled to get free.

He drew her to her feet. She broke loose, then almost nose-dived again as her ridiculous heels wobbled.

"Steady," he said, putting out a hand to hold her.

"Get off me."

Her words cut like a whip, and he obeyed, palms up, and took a step away.

"Lexi, are you okay?" Mrs. Franklin, the wife of the Bible college director, wrapped an arm around the woman.

"I want to go," the woman said.

"Jackson, thank you," Mrs. Franklin said warmly.

"No problem." When it looked like the rude redhead wasn't going to offer thanks, he drawled, "I think you need some new shoes, Miss Lexi."

Her eyes snapped to him, and he bit back a smile as it became obvious she was trying to figure out what to say. "You think?"

Whoa. This copperhead had some bite.

He studied her a moment longer, then dipped his chin. "I guess I won't be seeing you around."

"Good guess." She added a tight smile.

"Lexi," Mrs. Franklin murmured.

The green eyes checked out the heavens, and he was fairly certain he heard the faintest sigh. "Thank you."

"Oh, you're more than welcome," he said, molasses in his voice, then adding for good measure, "ma'am."

Ha. Just as he suspected, her nostrils flared at that last word, and her chin rose, revealing more of the wispy spotted scarf around her neck. With the scarf and the shirt and the heels she was kinda giving vibes of that 1950s chick, Audrey someone, whose movies his mom liked to watch. But that get-up must be pretty warm in these June temperatures. No wonder sweat was sliding down her forehead.

"Aren't you hot?"

She blinked. "I beg your pardon?"

He realized how that sounded, how he should've emphasized the question in his statement, and cleared his throat. "Wait, I didn't mean it like that."

Her mouth fell open.

Whoa. This day was getting better and better.

She took a wobbling step back, which forced her to clutch the arm of Mrs. Franklin. "Mum, can we please go now?"

Mum? There was a certain classy sound about her voice that drew him to hide another smile. She was like a rich kid, unaware her manners might strike some as disrespectful, but strangely charming nonetheless. And the fact she was Peter and Lynette Franklin's daughter meant he'd show her how things should be done round here. With courtesy, like they'd always shown him.

"Lexi, I don't think you've met Jackson Reilly, have you?" her mother said.

Jackson recognized the peacemaker and stuck out his hand. "Pleased to meet you."

Lexi eyed him then his hand, then shook it for the briefest moment. "Hello."

Her fingers released, but his didn't want to. He made himself let go.

"Lexi just arrived here from Australia," her mom said.

"Is that so?" He smiled. "Well, that's gotta be exciting, coming all the way here."

The way her lips pressed together, and she offered the barest nod, it didn't seem like she agreed.

At least he'd tried. "Well, I sure hope you enjoy your time here in Trinity Lakes."

"Thanks."

"Bye, Mrs. Franklin."

"Goodbye, Jackson."

"See you around, Ms. Franklin," he said to the daughter. "Ma'am," he added, biting back a grin.

Her gaze narrowed, but he didn't stay to watch, turning to see Ellie instead. "Ready?"

She mouthed a "wow" at him, then nodded, shooting a half smile in the direction of the Aussie, before taking his arm as they walked down the path. Lunch today was at Joe's Diner, the best eating place in town. His stomach was already twisting at the thought of the Trinity special.

"What was that?" she asked as soon as they were clear of being overheard.

"What was what?" he asked.

"I have never seen you act like that before."

"You mean superhero tough?" Jackson asked, flexing an arm.

"Stop it. You're embarrassing yourself. People are still watching." She peered over her shoulder. "She's still watching."

He was sorely tempted to look back, too. Oh, hang it. He pivoted, and the redhead's gaze instantly shifted away. A chuckle rumbled through his chest as they crossed the street. Two more doors, then goodbye hunger, hello heaven.

"Wow," Ellie said again. "Well, this'll be an interesting summer."

"What d'you mean?" He pushed the door open, holding it for Ellie as she passed through to the small foyer where guests sometimes had to wait. But the fact they were here early meant they could take their pick of booths.

"How long is she here for?" Ellie asked, choosing a booth by the front window and settling on the other side.

"Who?"

"Your Miss Fancy Pants."

Amusement lit again at the memory of the dirty knees. "She's a funny one, right?"

Her eyes rounded. "You like her."

"Come on. I don't even know her."

"You could," his sister said. "You should. It's been a long time since I've seen you act that way around a girl."

"What way?" He nodded to the server as they were handed menus and told about the specials of the day. It didn't matter what the laminated card said. He always ordered the same thing, the tradition as sure as Sundays in church. "Trinity burger with the works, thanks."

"Sure thing, Jackson." Marlene Holden didn't ever bother writing it down. "And the usual?"

"What would Sunday be without my chocolate shake?" He grinned.

"Such a child," his sister muttered.

"You know it." His smile widened as she ordered. His gaze traveled out the window. Sure enough, some of the other younger folk from church were making their way to the diner. This, his one brief chance to relax and connect with others away from the ranch, was a time he always savored. In two hours he'd be back checking fences, dealing with cattle, dealing with Mom. Considering how hard he worked, nobody could blame him for the chance to burn off some steam and play hooky.

"So …" Ellie said, drawing his attention again. "Before the others get here, are you going to give me a straight answer?"

"A straight answer about what?"

She rolled her eyes, and he lifted a hand motioning for Jasper Cohen, Josh Ladan and Brandon Taylor to join them.

"A straight answer about why you were flirting," she hissed.

"Flirting?"

She nodded, her lips lifting as his friends drew close. "Jackson Reilly, gettin' his flirt on."

"Eloise." He drew the word out with subtle warning.

Laughter rippled as Jasper slid in next to Ellie, giving her a grin before his attention turned to Jackson. "Did I hear right? Jackson was flirting? This I have to see."

"You could've, if you'd been in church today." Ellie's brows rose.

"Don't look at me like that," Jasper protested. "We had to take Bess to the vet."

"Uh huh."

"Come on now, Ellie. It took ages for Doc Martin to set her right."

Talk about flirting. The way Ellie and Jasper danced around each other was enough to make him wonder what needed to happen before Ellie finally decided to go out on a date.

"You were flirting?" Jasper asked, once he, Josh and Brandon had ordered. Jasper's family owned the hardware store two streets away.

"Trying to, anyway." Ellie smirked. "Seemed to mostly consist of showing off his muscles."

Laughter rippled from the others. "And we missed it?" Josh asked.

"Now that's not fair." Jackson shook his head. "I couldn't help it if she stumbled straight into my arms."

"Not that she looked like she enjoyed staying there," his sister said.

That was true. And a mite off-putting.

"You better work on your technique," Jasper said.

"I'm just fine, thank you. I don't have time for making pretty with the ladies."

"Who is this chick?" Josh asked. He might be the pastor's son, but he didn't always seem to pay close attention to things. "Is she pretty?"

"She's okay." Jackson shrugged. "Not really my type."

"This gets more interesting. I didn't know Jackson had a type. Did you?" he asked Brandon and Jasper.

"No, sir."

Ellie's grin seemed to split her face. "I'd say the way Jackson held her like they were in some fancy dance move sure made it look like he had a type."

"Want to demonstrate for me?" Jasper asked, wiggling his brows.

Jackson frowned and was about to object when Marlene returned with their meals.

What was the point of all this worry? Miss Franklin had made her opinion clear. And yeah, while he might find her strangely appealing, she'd made it clear she wanted nothing more to do with him. Which was fine. He didn't have time to chase a woman anyway.

CHAPTER TWO

Was there any job more satisfying than cleaning? Lexi hung up the last of the sheets on the washing line, surveying her morning's efforts. Trinity Lakes Bible College might have an industrial-sized dryer, but nothing beat the smell of freshly dried sheets ... not to mention the environmental benefits of using free sunshine instead of electricity. Today's warm, sunny weather almost had her thinking of life back home, those glorious days when she used to jog along the paths beside the beach, listening to the waves, feeling the salt-laden air freshen her cheeks. And while the ocean was hundreds of miles away, maybe she would get a chance to put her feet in the lake this afternoon. Now the students had left for the semester, she was here with her parents and a few other staff members for several weeks until the summer sessions began. That meant helping her parents give the college buildings the spring clean they couldn't do during semester. But even though it was often hard physical work, there was something gladdening about scrubbing dirt away and seeing surfaces sparkle, like they couldn't when the students were here. It was certainly different to nursing.

Her spirits dipped, but she refused to go there. It would take a miracle for her to feel like she could work in that field again. And given that God had used a miracle to keep her alive, she didn't want to beg for another.

She pegged the last of the sheets to the line—nothing said comfort like fresh sheets—and gazed down the hill to where the lake sparkled in the summer sun. This really was a pretty part of the world, something she'd enjoy exploring a little more in the upcoming weeks. After church on Sunday, Mum and Dad had taken her to a little café right in the heart of town. The Bellbird Café was a little pocket of Australiana in the middle of this Hallmark-worthy town. The background music with the tinkling sound of bellbirds had surprised her at first, before Dad had explained the place was owned by Aussie expats who had moved here fifteen years ago, bringing good coffee and Australian treats like lamingtons and vanilla slices to the population of Trinity Lakes. It was only patriotic to sample them, and she could now attest it was as good as anything she'd had from back home.

Home.

The word seemed foreign to her. Mum and Dad were here. And all she thought she wanted in Australia had been shattered just over three months ago. Now she felt this strange sense of drifting, like she didn't know where she fitted anymore. Being half American probably did that to a person, one's identity never fully secured. A foot on two continents, but never really planted. Instead, floating free like a twig in a stream.

"Lexi?"

She turned. "Hey, Mum."

"It's a gorgeous view, isn't it?"

"Lovely." Her heart was at ease for the first time in weeks.

"Thanks for all your help. I didn't expect you to do it all."

"I didn't expect to be lazing around on the couch, eating peeled grapes, so I guess we're even."

Her mother laughed. "It's a big place, isn't it?"

"It's great, but yeah. I can see why you need so many staff." The late Victorian building's three stories of timber and brick required a lot of cleaning, especially when the newer dormitories were factored in as well.

"We really appreciate them, but I know they've all earned a break. Speaking of, are you almost finished here? I was wondering if you'd like to come into town with me. I need to get some groceries and could do with another pair of hands."

"Sure."

The drive to the store wound through rolling hills covered in grapevines, bright green in the summer sun. Her father said the local vineyards produced some nice wines, but she'd never been a drinker, so that was something she'd have to take other people's word for.

The road passed a thriving outdoor activity park, garish signs announcing water slides and miniature golf and other fun summer activities. The packed parking lot suggested it was popular with locals and tourists. The car descended and crossed a bridge, then they navigated through the historic part of town to a large supermarket.

They found a cart, her mother handed her a list, and they began the joy of trawling up and down the aisles. It still surprised her how much mathematics such visits required, changing weights and volume measures from metric to American. Fortunately, their grocery needs weren't too high, and they were soon loading goods into the back of the station wagon.

"Barb?"

Lexi paused as her mother waved at a passing customer, hitching a smile to her dial as the lady glanced at her then started talking to Mum. Okay, so the other day at church had not been her finest hour. She cringed again, remembering how she must've appeared, all snooty and haughty like a spoiled princess. That wasn't her. But in that moment when the cowboy had held her—had rescued her—she had frozen as memories of the attack flared. Pasting politeness over her fear had proved a sorry effort, but it was the best she could do. For he'd held her in a way that made every pore freeze in memory—

"What do you think, Lexi? You'd like to do that, wouldn't you?"

"Sorry. What was the question?" She shook off the mental fog.

"Barb and Hank are hosting a barbecue on Thursday night and invited you. It'd be a great way to meet some of the other young people around here." Her mother's eyes held hope.

Lexi released air through her teeth. Maybe this would be a way to improve upon that first impression. Although she'd be super happy to never encounter Jackson Reilly again. Not that she would normally have a problem with talking to a handsome man, but the fact he seemed amused by her rudeness made her unsure. She had never known how to deal gracefully with people she sensed were laughing at her.

"Your father will be away speaking at a fishing camp, and I'll be at book club, and while you'd be welcome at that, I suspect you'd enjoy yourself more at Barb's."

Ah, the pinch of obligation. What choice did she have with Barb looking at her expectantly? Apparently, her problems with exiting social situations gracefully wasn't restricted to Sundays.

"That sounds good. When and where? What can I bring?"

"Oh, honey, you don't need to bring a thing," Barb said. "I'm sure your mom will be able to tell you where we are. And it's nothing fancy. Just a pool party. I'm sure you know how to swim, being an Aussie."

"A pool party?" She glanced at her mother and shook her head slightly. She couldn't do that. Not anymore.

"It will be a good chance to get to know others," her mother said. "You don't have to swim."

"Goodness, no. It'd take a miracle for me to put on a swimsuit again," Barb said with a hearty chuckle. "Not that that would be a problem for you, Lexi."

Except that it was. Swimming, like so many other things, had been stolen from her on that last night of February. How bizarre that something as simple as going to the beach now held all sorts of questions, demanding answers she didn't know how to give. And even the fact there *was* a question made her tense. Was she really that vain now, or had she always been?

Still, she hadn't come all this way to let the shadows of the past impede her from her future. "That sounds fun," she said. "Thank you."

She pasted on another smile. See? She could do nice. And maybe the night would go well. Especially if she didn't have any more run-ins with the man who'd made her feel so uncomfortable last Sunday.

NUMBERS WERE ABOUT to fry his brain. Unlike some people—his younger brother, Cooper came to mind, as did Liam Darcy, Olivia's grandson, from next door—Jackson had always felt like he and math were engaged in an ongoing battle. He liked his lists, and could check off boxes with the best of them, but struggling to wrestle ranch income to meet expenditure left him longing to give up the fight. He pushed the rolling chair away from the cluttered desk and glanced out the window, where a haze of yellow green shimmering off the distant hills suggested they'd need rain soon. A sigh escaped, one he was glad nobody was around to hear, as he sure as heck didn't want to be explaining himself to anyone. Ellie didn't seem to know a personal boundary when it smacked her in the face, and he had zero intention of adding to Mom's stress. *Lord, heal her.*

The prayer lifted from his heart but sometimes he wasn't sure it went much higher than the ceiling. Sure, God heard his every prayer, but sometimes He seemed to take an awful long time to answer. But deep within, he knew that God was faithful, just like Peter Franklin had shared on Sunday in his reminder to keep a focus on thankfulness. And Jackson *was* thankful, as he'd seen God's faithfulness, time after time. And just as God would soon bring an answer to the ranch's financial troubles—no, challenges—so God would also help with his mother's health battles too. "In Jesus' name," he prayed aloud.

He pushed himself upright, hating the confines of this former bedroom now turned office. He'd much rather be out on Arrow riding the fences, checking the stock. But Jose and Felipe's pay grade meant they earned the right to live in the saddle way more often than him, while he got the joy of wrestling numbers inside this box of a room until it felt like his eyeballs were going to bleed.

His phone rang, and he eyed it like it was a rattlesnake, wondering if he should answer. "Such a tough guy," he muttered to himself and scooped it up and answered. "This is Jackson."

"Ah, Jackson." The voice was vaguely familiar. "This is Millie from First National. Is now a good time?"

Was any time a good time to talk to the bank? "I don't have long—"

"I won't keep you. I know you're busy, especially at this time of the year."

If she knew that, why didn't she get to the point? "What is this about?" Directness was his middle name. Even if he had a fairly solid idea about what she was going to say. *Please God.*

"I know that some of our mail has been, shall we say, misplaced over the years—"

Misplaced, misdirected, whatever.

"—so I thought I'd call. I'm sure you'd appreciate being saved a trip to town."

"I do appreciate that, thank you." The words came out tight, impatient, even as he shot for as much politeness as he could, as his gut tensed. *Please God, please God, please ...*

"I'm sorry, but your application for a loan extension has been denied."

He closed his eyes, the word beating into his soul. Denied. Denied? What the heck was he going to do now?

"Considering the mortgage has already been extended once, the bank truly is in no position to offer further credit unless and until we know there is a guarantee of payment within the parameters of our initial contract. I'm afraid we both know you have not met your legal obligations to date."

He swallowed. Was her slight emphasis on *legal* a hint that this could be about to get ten times worse? "Millie, you know things have been tough lately. We just need a little more time."

"I'm sorry, Mr. Reilly—"

"We're back to formalities now?" That never boded well.

"—but having been the one to personally review the application, I had to conclude it did not meet our criteria for automatic approval."

His eyes closed, his finger clenched, and he was sorely tempted to kick something. Then that second-last word filtered into his brain again. "You said automatic approval."

"Yes."

"Does that mean there are grounds for alternative approval?"

"I'm not sure what you mean."

"Is there a way I can amend the application to earn the bank's approval?"

There was a short pause. "As explained in the policy document you read before filling out the application, there is no guarantee that an application will meet with success. So I'm sorry, but unless you can come up with an alternative option that will prove financially viable, the answer will still be no."

"But Brutus is destined to be the top breeding bull in the county."

"But he isn't now," her voice was patient, like he was a little kid, and not someone he'd shared a freshman English class with fifteen years ago. "If you can get that side of the business going, then well and good. If not, well, I'm afraid we'll need to consider what options remain."

"What options do remain?" Man, he hated the whining sound in his voice.

"I'm afraid your options are being increasingly more limited, but such is the case for anyone who has extended their mortgage to the extent you have. If you hadn't bought that new machinery last year—"

Machinery that meant he could grade his road after heavy rain or snow and not have to wait for the county to fix it.

"—then perhaps things wouldn't be so dire. But what's done is done, and unless you find a solution in the next month or so, then you may need to consider whether you should sell off a parcel of your land."

Now he really wanted to swear.

"I'm sorry, Jackson," she said. "We'll be in touch, okay?"

"Can't wait." He stabbed at the phone to hang up, but even that piece of childish spite was denied him as he saw she had already ended the call.

He was sorely tempted to throw the phone across the room, but didn't, knowing he would then have to buy a new one. And that, like everything else, was something he couldn't afford.

What was he going to say? What was he going to do? *God, help me.*

He shifted to face the view and stretched back in the chair, extending his arms and legs to full capacity, rolling his shoulders to release the tension. But nothing could truly release the pressure within. He'd known things were bad. But this bad? How could little Millie Avery be so uncaring, like she'd forgotten he used to flirt with her in school?

His fingers dug into his hair, his mind spinning. What would he do? What would the others say? What would his brothers say? He gritted his teeth as the old envies rose. Dermott, who'd escaped while he could. Mitchell, the golden child, off living his dream of pro sports and reveling in all the money and fame that afforded him. Then there was Cooper, brainy as they came, who'd turned up his nose at working the land to chase dollars in tech industries. Leaving poor Ellie stuck here, unable to chase her dream of archeology, while Jackson had apparently run his dream of ranch ownership—of being the only Reilly to keep the family legacy going—straight into the ground. How could he ever admit to them what he could barely admit to himself: that he wasn't the ranchman he'd dreamed of being since he was a boy. That he'd failed.

Nope. No way was he going to admit his failure to them. No way would he ever live it down. There had to be a way to make things work.

A hollow gnawing feeling swept through his chest, panic rising. Would they have to sell? What would that mean for Mom? She was the reason they kept so many things the same. What would it mean for Ellie and options for her future?

"Ahem."

He spun in his chair to see Ellie grinning at the door.

"Sorry for interrupting. That looks like a new method for head massage. It must work, because you seemed miles away and didn't hear me knocking."

"Fiji would be nice, but I wasn't miles away. Right here in fact." He grimaced.

"You look like you need some fun."

"Fun? What's that?"

"Aww, poor Jackson, locked up in here like a martyr. Poor you. Hey, I just got an invite for a party at the Andersson's on Thursday. Want to come?"

After the phone call he'd had, all he wanted was to stay focused on work, and try to squeeze every last dollar from this place. But the hopeful look on Ellie's face was something he hadn't seen for a while, so he tamped down the anxiety and pasted on a smile. "No promises, but maybe?"

"I'll take that as a yes."

"You always take anything I say and run with it."

"Because I know you love me."

True.

"Is there anything I can do?"

He sniffed the air, where a delectable scent promised there'd be a nice end to this day. "Whatever you're cooking, keep on doing."

She made a face. "It's stew. Like you haven't had that a hundred times before. No, what is it? What's got you looking so worried?"

"I'm not worried."

"Liar."

"Okay, I am worried." He picked up a plastic sticky tape dispenser and tossed it between his hands. "I'm worried about when you're going to finally get a real job, one you actually want to do."

Maybe her wages could contribute to the ranch if she had a real job. He could charge board. Great. Look at him, squeezing his own siblings for cash.

"I don't need a real job. I've got one right here."

"Nice try. You and I both know this is a temporary gig."

The teasing look drained from her eyes. "What is it, Jackson? You look stressed. And I'm not used to seeing you stressed. The others, yes. But you ..."

He bit his lip. When had his baby sister grown up and grown so smart? She might be twenty-four, but sometimes she seemed years older.

She drew closer. "Is it the ranch?"

"When is it not?"

Her nose wrinkled. "I'm sorry. Is there something I can do?"

"I know you're doing the best you can. It's not like you ever spend big." He eyed her clothes, the stained t-shirt and years-old denim cutoffs. If he was doing things as he should, she'd be getting a new wardrobe every year, like other girls. But he wasn't. Guilt strummed his chest.

"I can help more. Maybe do some of the range riding."

"I don't want you out there alone."

"You let Felipe ride out alone, and he's younger than me."

"And he's not my little sister."

"Not that little, thank you."

His jaw clenched. Nope. She wasn't so little anymore. And if he were a better brother, he'd be making sure she was out in the world getting her chance to know men she wasn't related to. Or men she'd known all her life, like Jasper. She'd have a chance at a future, at marriage, a family. Even if he couldn't.

"Come on. Don't treat me as a child. Tell me what's going on."

Maybe he should give a hint of what was going on. Break the ice slowly as it were. "That was the bank."

"How is Millie these days?"

"Not as friendly as I'd like."

"Ouch. She turned you down?"

"I didn't ask her for a date."

"Don't be stupid. I know that. I also know who you should ask for a date." She waggled her eyebrows.

"Stop right there," he said, even as a tiny part of him wanted to know more. "I'm talking about the bank, remember?"

"Fine." She little-girl pouted. "What did mean Millie have to say?"

"She's not mean, just doing her job, but ..." A sigh escaped before he could stop it.

"I'm sorry, Jackson."

"Yeah, well, if we can get Brutus to finally do his thing, maybe we'll keep afloat."

Her eyes rounded. "Things are that bad?"

"It's not that bad." Man. He hadn't wanted to scare her. "Just things aren't as good as they could be. I mean, it'd be nice to have the money to send you to Greece, but sorry, no can do."

"What? You mean I can't go on this trip I've never once thought about? You dream crusher."

"That's me." He forced out a smile. "Mr. Dream Crusher, right here."

Tease faded as her face took on that worried look he'd seen way too often recently. "Are we okay? Do we need to tighten our belts some more?"

He'd need to get out the nail gun and pierce another couple of holes in their belts for them to tighten anymore. "We'll be fine." *In Jesus name.*

She studied him a long moment, then finally nodded. "Speaking of fine, have you spoken to Mom recently?"

He shook his head. "I've been in here all day and missed her last night at dinner. Why?"

"I think we need to take her to the doctor again. She's acting kind of weird."

"How?"

"I don't know. Just a bit off. I haven't seen her like this for years."

A bit off.

The words struck like a bullet through his heart. He remembered the first time he'd heard that description of his mom. He'd only been six at the time, when Ellie was just a baby, and his mom, his poor mom, had been abandoned by her husband. She had carried on for many years, being strong, running the ranch and her kids, somehow managing to save enough to send Mitchell off to hockey camps, but he still recalled hearing those words for the first time, when he'd seen his mother in a different light, and realized she wasn't the superwoman they'd always assumed.

"She's a bit off," Mrs. Ingalls had whispered at church.

The words had sparked Jackson and his brothers in different ways. Dermott had tried to show his love by building an overly grand stone wall at the front entrance to the driveway. Mitchell refused to go to church, saying it was full of hypocrites, and was soon lost to the world of hockey, a scholarship leading him to live away in North Dakota in his mid-teens. Jackson had determined to live here and help his mom in any way possible. The fact that meant he got to stay on the ranch doing what he loved was a bonus. He'd do anything to relieve his mom of concern, so people like Mrs. Ingalls would never say she was "off" again.

But even he wasn't so stuck in denial that he hadn't noticed the lost feeling that had shrouded his mom in those first few weeks had returned. She was keeping to her room again, not even bothering to show up for every meal. Lethargy seemed to have taken over her bones, making her seem smaller, skinnier than he remembered.

Maybe his efforts to help her and keep her safe only proved he was a failure at that too.

He shook his head at himself, conscious his long silence now meant Ellie was looking at him funny. "Do you want to take her to the doctor?"

She nodded. "He might have some new medication to give her."

"Hope so. Maybe ask him to come visit."

They already owed the doc—and the vet—for plenty of house calls. A little extra on the tally couldn't hurt.

God, help Brutus get it together.

Everything was riding on their stud bull finally being able to do what he was created for. If that worked, then all—well, most —of their problems would be solved. And maybe he could afford to buy Ellie a new dress.

CHAPTER THREE

"Lexi, are you sure you'll be okay?" her mother asked, brow pleated.

Lexi glanced at the single-story timber home, with a number of vehicles parked out the front, and slowly opened the station wagon's front passenger door. "I'll be fine." What was the worst that could happen? "You have fun with the ladies at the book club."

"I imagine we'll be finished far sooner than you. I sometimes get the impression they'd rather meet to gossip and have cupcakes than actually read the book."

"Probably depends on the book," Lexi said, earning her mother's chuckle.

"I'm proud of you, Lexi," Mum said.

Why did those words fuel both irritation and pride? Yes, she mightn't like being addressed like a child, but she was also glad someone recognized the Big Deal it was to actually be here tonight. And it *was* a big deal, meeting strangers, doing small talk, acting braver than she was. Once upon a time, she wouldn't have blinked. Now, every new thing held the possibility of danger.

She swung her scarf around so the ends flounced at the front, then carefully retrieved the pavlova from the back seat, and straightened.

"You could still have a swim, you know."

"I know." She'd even brought her swimsuit in case the spirit of brave fell upon her. Unlikely, but you never knew.

"Enjoy yourself, okay? And call us when you want a ride home."

"Yes, Mum," she said obediently, earning her a wrinkled nose and a chuckle before her mother waved and drove away.

Lexi drew in a deep breath. Okay. Friendly. She could do this. Even if it felt like her mother had arranged this like she might arrange a play date for a five-year-old. Oh, who was she kidding? Mum *had* arranged this like Lexi was little better than a child.

She walked up the garden path—no wobble-inducing cobblestones here—and knocked.

No answer.

She knocked again, then put her ear to the door and listened. It sounded like music, and all the cars suggested something was happening here tonight. Maybe they just couldn't hear her.

One more knock, then—

"Can I help you, ma'am?" A male voice sounded behind her.

"Oh!" The pavlova slid from her grasp and landed on the rosebush near the front door. "Oh no!" She looked up into deep brown eyes, her breath catching again. "You."

"You." Jackson Reilly smiled.

So judging from her pulse skitters, her heart might not have got the memo to find this man unappealing. Apparently her senses could not lie. But as she glanced down at the ruined remains of her dessert, she knew she wouldn't follow through. The man was married, for goodness sake. And even though she might've felt the strangest tug of attraction right now, the fact his wife stood there, smiling at the scene like she thought Lexi endearingly clumsy, did not give a girl any confidence about how to act.

Except maybe like this.

She rose, picked up her dignity along with the plate, and smiled at the woman. "Hello, I'm Lexi."

The brunette's grin revealed sweet dimples. "I'm Ellie Reilly."

See? Married.

Lexi's gaze slid from Ellie to Jackson then rushed back to the door again. "So … what time was this supposed to start?"

Jackson's arm snaked past her shoulder as he twisted the door handle and pushed it open. "Five thirty."

"But it's almost an hour later," she said, horrified. Forget trying to be sociable. Maybe she'd be better off going home.

"Don't worry about that. Barb and Hank are pretty relaxed. They probably haven't even started eating yet."

Ellie's words drew Lexi's focus back to her lopsided dessert. The cream had slid off, the fruit lay askew, and there was a size-able difference in thickness between the two sides.

"What do you call that?" Jackson asked.

For a moment, she wasn't sure if he was being sarcastic or not. She decided to give him the benefit of the doubt. "It was a pavlova."

"Until Big Mouth here scared you," Ellie said.

"I bet it still tastes good," he said, eyes still on her.

She swallowed. "How do you know it tastes good?"

"If it's anything like the ones they sell at the Bellbird café, it'll be good."

"Jackson has a sweet tooth." Ellie said in a mock stage whis-per. "If there's sugar involved, he's in."

"I see."

"Do you?" Ellie said, glancing at the tall man. "Because I think it's unfair that someone can eat as much junk food as he does and still look like that. Don't you?"

O-kay. What was the right answer to a question like that? "We should probably go in."

"Yeah, I need a swim." Jackson gestured for them both to go inside. Lexi passed into a carpeted entry hall tastefully decorated in muted pastel tones, with a large photograph of Barb and presumably Barb's husband taking pride of place over a hall table that held an old-fashioned telephone.

"Don't worry about your dessert," Ellie said. "I bet you my firstborn that Barb has gallons of cream and strawberries you can add on top."

"Okay."

Clutching her misshapen offering, Lexi followed them through to a kitchen that formed part of an open-plan living area. Glass doors led outside to a large kidney-shaped pool.

"Lexi, you came!" Barb said, face alight as she drew near. "Oh, how wonderful. And look, you've made some friends already."

"Sure has," Ellie said, tossing Lexi a grin, which bounced around Lexi's heart before she returned it with one of her own.

Friendship. Lexi used to be better at it. But she didn't know how to do simple friendship since the attack. Everyone seemed to keep moving on, while she'd kind of stalled. It was only to be expected, people would say—her parents, her pastors, her counsellors. But she didn't want to expect this anymore. She wanted new and different, hence her decision to leave the past behind and escape to east Washington state. Except sometimes it seemed she might never escape the past's clutches. Like her overreaction on Sunday.

"And what have we got here?" Barb asked, eyeing Lexi's dessert, trying and failing to hide her doubt.

"Pavlova."

"Upside-down pavlova." Jackson placed two bottles on the table. "My special creation. Sorry."

"I feel there is a story I don't have time to hear. Want to pretty it up with some more strawberries and cream?"

"Yes, please," Lexi said.

Barb retrieved the ingredients from the fridge and motioned for Lexi to do her thing.

"Jackson, can you bring the drinks outside?" Barb left the room, and Jackson followed with the drinks. His broad back seemed to block half the light as he left.

"You gonna swim today?" Ellie asked.

Lexi's attention swung back to her task, but not before she noticed Ellie wore a small smile, like she was used to women ogling her husband. Oh, to be so secure. What were they talking about again? That's right. Swimming.

"Probably not." She might be making some steps towards courage, but one couldn't get carried away. Even if she did hate the feeling of sitting on the sidelines. Even if the teenage Lexi had promised herself to never stop having a go at things like swimming like so many older women seemed to. What kind of message did that send to their children? It was like cutting your hair short when you turned fifty, as though long hair was reserved for the young. Nope. Not gonna play.

"I don't swim either," Ellie said, watching as Jackson greeted some people then headed to the pool. "Jackson thinks I'm crazy, but I've never been confident in the water."

"Swimming isn't for everyone," Lexi said.

Although it seemed to be for everyone else who was here. The guests looked to range from late teens through to early thirties, all enjoying cooling off from today's heat by swimming, diving, jumping, splashing others. Yeah, coming tonight sure was a great idea. Could she leave yet?

But something urged her to stay, maybe because she'd always been a glutton for punishment.

She finished redecorating the pavlova, stored it in the fridge, and headed outside with Ellie where they found a couple of wicker chairs in the corner of the pool area. Ellie grabbed a packet of chips, and Lexi joined her, propping her sunglasses on her nose.

"So," Ellie said, "Tell me about yourself."

Somehow it seemed easier to share about her life with someone who clearly knew little about her. Instead of focusing on the last three months, she could share the things she wanted others to know. So Lexi shared about her studies, her nursing career, and answered questions about life in Australia.

"That sounds awesome. I think Jackson would love to visit one day."

Lexi coughed, almost choking on a fake sour cream-flavored potato chip.

"You okay? Here, have a drink." Ellie passed her a plastic tumbler of brightly colored soda, and she gulped it down.

"Hey, Ellie." A handsome man sat opposite them, nodded a greeting at Lexi, then focused entirely on Ellie. Huh. Lexi wondered what Jackson would have to say about a man speaking to his wife like that. She glanced back at the pool, in time to see his tanned broad chest rise from the water. She swallowed. Looked away. Why was Ellie focused on this other man and not her husband?

"So. Lexi."

She glanced up, zeroing in on a chest that said hello to every one of her senses. Then she had to swallow and whisk her gaze away to the hills gleaming yellow in the evening sun.

"Don't you swim either?"

"I do." She knew she sounded defensive and tried to soften it with a smile. "I just didn't feel like swimming today."

Jackson picked up a towel and dried his hair then wrapped it around his neck so it draped over his chest. She was glad. She shouldn't be paying attention to his pecs. "So have you forgiven me yet?"

"Forgiven—oh. Of course. Yeah. Sorry."

His smile slid up half his face. "I'm glad you came today. Ellie was glad to meet you."

"Ellie's really nice." Even if she was still talking to the other guy and hadn't paid Jackson a lick of attention.

"I was wondering—"

"Hey, Jackson. Dude. Is this her?"

Some man Lexi had never seen before grinned at her, then at Jackson.

Wait. Had he been talking about her? Judging from the wry glance he shot at his friend, it seemed the answer was yes. Which begged the question—why? Heat rose up her cheeks as she wondered what he might've said. That she was the clumsiest person he'd ever met? The rudest? She ducked her head, glanced at her phone, and wondered if it was too early to call her mother.

"Lexi, meet Jasper."

She peeked up. Managed a small smile. "Pleased to meet you."

Jasper's grin didn't cause sparkles inside like his friend's had. His *married* friend, she told herself firmly. "Hi."

Jasper seemed to take this as invitation to join them on the nearby wicker lounge and talk to Jackson. The man from Barb's photo inside called "grub's up," triggering a rush to the barbecue.

She wasn't hungry, and the thought of all those strangers she'd need to make small talk with meant she'd happily wait a while longer. So she tuned out, her gaze drifting back to the pool, which had by now emptied of most bodies, except ...

She leaned forward, peering more closely. Was that—? No. Surely someone else would've noticed. She stood anyway, edging closer to the water. Then gasped, and tossed the plastic tumbler to the ground and jumped in.

———

"Lexi? What are—?" Ellie's words dissolved into a shriek.

Jackson's attention snapped to the woman at the bottom of the pool, her arm crooked around a lifeless-looking body as she slowly propelled herself to the surface.

Her head broke the surface, and she was spluttering. "Help me!"

Jackson dived in. Two seconds later, he relieved her of her burden, doing his best to keep the boy's nose and mouth out of the water. "It's Jordan," he yelled to the others standing watching, jaws dropped, horrified. "Call 911."

He reached the side where willing hands drew Jordan up and onto the ground, and someone pounded the teen on the back.

"No!" Barb screamed and rushed to her son's side. "What happened? Jordan? Oh, my baby!"

"He was in the water," Lexi said, gasping, from behind him. "Who knows CPR?"

"I sorta—"

"Move." She pushed past, elbowing him aside and dropped to her knees, her t-shirt and shorts plastered wetly to her skin. She rolled Jordan onto his side and drew open his mouth. "Come on."

Water trickled, but there was still no response. She tugged Jordan to lie on his back, laid two fingers under his nose, her brow wrinkling.

"What can I do?" Jackson said. "Give me a job."

"Get them back," she said, not looking at him. "He needs space, and he'll freak out if everyone's here in his face."

She repositioned Jordan's head, then leaned down to listen, ear to his chest, then measured two hand spans in, interlocking the heels of her hands as she commenced fast, hard compressions on his chest to the beat of "Stayin' Alive."

After counting to thirty, she tilted back Jordan's forehead, lifted his chin forward and leaned close, and pushed air from her mouth to his, then resumed pressing his chest.

"Here, let me." Jackson moved beside her and breathed for the boy he'd known all his life.

"Give him two breaths."

Jackson breathed again. This time the boy coughed, choked, then turned his head away as more water spilled from his mouth in a series of gasps.

"Get him a towel to warm him up." Lexi lifted Jordan's head slightly, soothing him and encouraging him to expel all the water. "Everyone needs to get back again and give him room."

Jackson sat back on his heels as the others obeyed, adrenaline fading as he watched the woman whose calmness had saved Jordan's life carry on her ministrations. If she hadn't noticed Jordan …

Guilt struck. How many of them had been here? And Lexi had been the only person to notice? His skin crawled. He'd always prided himself on being observant. A man had to be observant to run a ranch—missing a coyote's tracks today could mean missing several sheep in upcoming days or weeks. But he hadn't been observant this evening. No. He'd been observant, but he'd been focused on the wrong things. Like wondering what the specific name was of the pretty color of Lexi Franklin's hair, and why she still wore a scarf around her neck on a blazing hot day.

He glanced at her now, the scarf hanging limply at her throat, the wet clothes she wore meaning she'd need a towel or jacket real soon. She obviously hadn't planned to go swimming.

He swallowed and pushed himself to his feet, trailing closer to Lexi as she spoke quietly to Barb and Hank, who were now hovering over Jordan.

"… will be here soon. You'll be okay." She gently rubbed Jordan's arm.

"Oh, thank you, thank you." Tears filled Barb's eyes, and Hank drew an arm around his wife. "I don't know what I would've done."

"I'm glad I was here." Then Lexi smiled.

Somehow her gaze drifted up to meet his, holding, connecting, as his gut kicked and his pulse roared. So that's what a genuine smile from Lexi looked like. He smiled back, and she startled, blinking, breaking the connection, turning as Ellie draped a towel around her shoulders.

A siren wailed through the air, flashing lights signaling the ambulance's arrival. Twenty minutes later, Jordan and his folks were headed to the tiny Trinity Lakes' hospital. Even though he seemed fine, Jocelyn and the other paramedic wanted to keep him in for observation.

Couples and singles traipsed to the door, leaving Jackson and Jasper to pick up the last of the party detritus. Having refused medical attention, Lexi sat on an outdoor lounge in the corner, her admirers from earlier having mostly faded away. Her offer to help clean up had been dismissed, with Jasper and others treating her like today's prom queen. But Jackson had noticed the way she'd stacked plastic cups anyway, as if sitting still was as much an anathema to her as it was to him.

"This is a party we won't forget in a hurry," Jasper muttered. "Thank God Lexi was here, huh?"

"She knew just what to do." Which, to be honest, kind of floored him. She certainly hadn't given off any cool, calm, collected vibes until now. His gaze sprung back to her, on the opposite side of the pool, out of hearing—he hoped. Judging from the expression she was now showing as Ellie continued talking, she was out of her comfort zone too.

"She was amazing," Jasper said.

Jackson glanced at him. Did the hardware heir have an interest there?

"But did you notice the scar?"

"What scar?"

"You probably didn't because you were too busy being an action hero."

Jackson rolled his eyes. "What scar?"

"On her neck, about here." Jasper drew a line across his throat. "It's not exactly little."

A scar? Is that why she wore scarves and high-necked tops? What had happened to her?

"Jackson?" Ellie tugged at his sleeve. "Would you mind if we go now?"

"Uh, sure."

"And can we take Lexi? She drowned her phone when she jumped in the pool, so I promised her I'd take her home."

Why did his heart leap at that thought? He strove for nonchalance. "Sure. Is she ready now?"

"I think she was ready to leave before she arrived," Ellie said wryly.

He'd noticed that reluctance as well. "Then let's go."

Maybe he'd learn some more clues about this increasingly fascinating lifesaving Australian.

CHAPTER FOUR

"Oh my gosh, Lexi. You were amazing! How did you know to do all that stuff?"

Lexi closed her eyes, glad Ellie couldn't see her from the front seat. "I'm a nurse, remember?"

"You were awesome."

The pickup slowed, and Lexi peeked to see Jackson was waiting at a red light while two pedestrians crossed the road.

"I still can't believe none of us noticed him," Jackson muttered.

Lexi swallowed and steered her gaze to the darkened park, the obelisk commemorating fallen soldiers lit in the night. Yeah, she couldn't believe that nobody had noticed Jordan either. But thank God she had. Maybe that was why she'd had that strange compulsion to stay. Her lips twisted. Far better a God-prompting than some wrong compulsion to see Jackson again. How could she have smiled at him like that? Especially when Ellie had proved to be so kind. She shivered and drew Ellie's borrowed jacket more firmly across her as he resumed driving.

The car filled with a strange quietness. Every so often Lexi sensed Jackson glance at her, but she kept her gaze steadfastly out the window, as if the evening lights of Trinity Lakes were the most fascinating thing ever.

"You're sure you don't want to go to the hospital?" he asked again.

"I don't need to. I'm a medical professional, and I know I'm okay."

"Right. Yeah. Of course."

She was technically okay health-wise. But the gut-squeezing moment in the pool and in the minutes afterwards had barely let her breathe and would doubtless eat into her hard-won peace of mind. Thank God her medical instincts had switched into overdrive, that all she'd done was simply a product of years of experience, both medically but also from surf lifesaving drills. She must've done dozens of pretend drills, but she could count actual resuscitations on one hand. Well, two hands now.

She glanced down at her blunt unpolished nails and grimaced, then winced again. Thank goodness Ellie had come to the rescue when she had, wrapping her in that towel. Until that moment she hadn't realized just how much she was revealing. Wet t-shirt contests weren't her scene.

Her hand drifted to her throat, and she readjusted the scarf, putting it back in place, remembering all the eyes, the questions, the intense attention. She'd never been one for the spotlight, and had retreated to a brand of shyness that too often left her second-guessing herself and other people's motives since the incident three months ago. She'd thought she'd left the shyness behind. Hadn't realized she'd brought it here, too.

Lexi's embarrassment dissipated in another wave of shame. How could she remain so focused on herself when a young man had almost died? *Lord, heal Jordan. Bring him to complete health, heal him and his parents' emotional trauma.* She swallowed. *And mine.*

"So, Bible college, huh?" Jackson said, as his truck climbed the hill.

"Yep." Maybe one-word answers could help her emotionally distance herself from him.

"It's a great school," Ellie said. "I wondered about studying there but couldn't afford it."

One of the complaints Dad often heard. But despite the costs being kept to a bare-bones minimum, Bible college, with Christian studies as the only focus, was often regarded by many as a frivolous luxury.

"Have you studied?" Lexi asked Ellie.

"Not really. I once did a semester of history online."

"History?"

"Yeah. I love archeology, and once thought I might like to work at the local museum, but the ranch kind of needs me."

Like the Bible college needed her, or so Dad said. "Family obligations, huh?"

A beat. Two. "Ellie is not obliged to work there." Jackson's voice held stiffness.

"Come on. What would you and Mom do without me? You know she'd never cope."

Ellie's mother was there too? And how could Ellie joke about leaving him? Lexi frowned.

"You okay back there?" Ellie asked.

"I'm fine."

"We're almost there," Jackson said, and she could tell from the curve in the road that he was right. It might've been a few years, but returning to Trinity Lakes was like slipping on old boots, and it hadn't taken long to refamiliarize herself with the bends, the bows, and hooks.

Like the hook of obligation.

She swallowed the disloyal thought as they passed the spotlit sign for Trinity Lakes Bible College and traveled the bumpy road. Dad had said he'd like to get the road graded, but that took money the college didn't have. And with no students for a few weeks, it wasn't a top priority.

"The road's a bit rough." Jackson said.

"Yep."

Another beat of silence passed. "I could maybe bring in some equipment to help fix it."

"Thanks. I'll mention it to my dad."

The three stories of the main building appeared, and a knot in her heart unraveled. For all the complexity of staying here, it had proved a respite from the outside world. And it would likely prove a respite from the difficult social complexities she now found herself in, which she couldn't blame on anyone else. It was simply what came from spending too long alone. One imagined things, got carried away, and struggled to differentiate between fact and fiction.

Jackson pulled the pickup outside the main doors, which were positioned under a pretentious porte-cochere that looked more suitable for a castle than a college devoted to teachings about a humble servant-King. Now, to get inside before her mother felt the need to investigate who had dared drive in so late at night.

"Thanks." She opened the door, carefully grasping the washed plate of the unfortunate pavlova. At least her disguise job in Barb's kitchen meant it had all been eaten, with some people—she might've noticed Jackson—returning for a second slice. "I appreciate the ride."

"No problem."

Jackson flashed another smile at her, and her heartbeat skittered again.

This was insane. She shifted from his view, going to speak to Ellie, who powered down the window. "Um, do you want your jacket now, or—"

"Keep it. For the moment, anyway. Hey, we'll have to have

you come visit the ranch sometime. What do you think, Jackson?"

He might've mumbled a "sure" but in truth, it didn't matter what his answer was. It was a solid no from her.

"Thanks, but I'll have to see how I go. It gets busy sometimes."

"But it's summer." Ellie's tone held a combination of disbelief and protest. "Don't all the students have a break?"

"There's still stuff to do." Lexi thought quickly. "Cleaning, and … stuff."

"Oh."

From the look on Ellie's face it didn't seem she was buying what Lexi was trying to sell. Had her blow-off been that obvious? And this, from the woman who had only been kind to her? "Thanks Ellie, I really do appreciate your offer. I better go—"

"Lexi?"

She closed her eyes for a moment then turned to face her mother. "Hi, Mum."

Her mother gasped. "What happened? Why didn't you call?"

"I ended up going for a swim after all. So did my phone. Ellie was kind enough to bring me home."

The engine died behind her, and a door opened. "Lexi was a hero tonight," Ellie said.

"She saved Jordan Andersson from drowning," Jackson's voice joined Ellie's praise.

"What?" Her mother looked from Lexi to the others then back again. "Is he okay?"

"The paramedics took him to hospital for observation," Ellie said.

"I just got a message from Hank." Jackson held up his phone. "He said Jordan has been released now."

"Oh, praise the Lord," her mother breathed.

"Amen," Ellie said.

Indeed.

"I'll message Barb as soon as I can. Poor woman. That must've been so frightening for her. It always is when one of your children is involved. I can remember—" Her mother glanced at Lexi, as if remembering what Lexi had made them promise not to say. "Anyway, darling, are you okay?"

"I'm fine. Really." Except for the fuss everyone was making.

"Oh my goodness. Well, praise God you were there in time. Jackson, Ellie, thank you so much for bringing Lexi home."

There was that five-year-old feeling again.

"The least we can do, ma'am."

Oh. So "ma'am" was actually Jackson's thing. He didn't say it to tease or be annoying.

"Please, come on in. I want to hear all about it. I'll make coffee or hot chocolate. I'm sure you all need something to warm you up."

Please, Mum, no.

But her mother wasn't looking at her. She was looking at the Reillys, as if Lexi's wishes didn't count.

"I'm afraid I can't stay," Jackson said. "Early morning duties at the ranch. Would love to though another time. I've always been curious about this place."

"You're welcome any time," Mum said warmly. "Isn't he, Lexi?"

She coughed. "Excuse me?" Was her mother seriously trying to fix her up with a married man? Wow. No words.

"And you too, of course, Ellie," Mum continued. "I appreciate you looking after poor Lexi here."

Like Lexi wasn't several years older than Ellie.

"I hope you'll visit us at the ranch soon," Ellie said. "I think it'll be fun."

Good thing she thought that. Trying to stay away from Jackson felt like it'd be torture. The hope in Ellie's eyes drew Lexi's smile wider than she wanted. "Thanks."

"Have a good sleep, Lexi," Jackson said. "You've earned it."

"You too." She pressed her lips up into a small smile and quickly looked away.

"Thanks again for dropping her home." Mum wrapped her arm around Lexi's shoulders. "Drive safe now."

"Yes, ma'am," Jackson said. "Bye Lexi."

Why did her heart throb at how he said her name? It wasn't like he said it any different to other people. "Bye." She smile-grimaced at Ellie. "Thanks again, Ellie."

Ellie's brow had a crease, and she moved close, forcing Mum to drop her arm as she took Lexi in a hug. "I don't know what Jackson has done to make you mad, but I hope you'll forgive him," she murmured. "I want us to be friends."

Lexi closed her eyes, hoping to hide the sudden rush of moisture. She drew in a deep breath through a clogged nose. "Sorry, I'm just tired. That's all."

"Good. Because I could really do with some girl company sometimes. My mom isn't always well."

Compassion surged. Perhaps she could consider this for Ellie's sake. "Maybe we could catch up for a coffee in town sometime." Town would be safe.

"Yeah, that could be good. But the offer to visit the ranch is always there. I think you'd have fun. There aren't too many ranches in Australia, right?"

"Not near the beach where I lived," Lexi admitted.

Ellie grinned. "Great! Well, I should get your number and— oh, you can't do that at the moment, can you?"

"Not until I get a new phone."

"Well, maybe I'll see you at church. You could visit us after church for lunch. That'd be good, wouldn't it?"

She swallowed. "Sure." Her voice sounded flatter than a squashed frog's.

"And don't worry about Jackson. I know he can be annoying at times. But I guess that's what brothers are for. I should know." She grimaced. "I've got four."

"Four brothers?"

Ellie sighed and drew back, counting on her fingers. "Dermott, Mitchell, Jackson and Cooper."

She blinked, and the world felt like it tipped on its axis. "Wait. Did you say Jackson is your brother?"

"Yeah. So please say you'll come to lunch on Sunday?"

She swallowed. Peeked at Jackson. "Uh, sure."

———

JACKSON TIGHTENED the brace wire in the fence, then pulled the wire sideways. His gloved hands felt the equal tension, so he knew his job was done. He straightened, stretching his back as he glanced across the low hills of their valley. *Their* valley was a slight misnomer. His friend and neighbor Liam Darcy might own the land to the west, but he didn't own the views, or the sunsets, or the way the hills held a purple shroud just before it rained.

He drew in a breath of fresh-cut hay and then released. One of his favorite scents, one that always made him think of summer. He drew in another breath, and for another precious moment the worries of the week slowed. He might not have the money or connections the Darcy family had, but this land had been Reilly land since long before old man Darcy first bought his spread, sixty years ago. Reillys had farmed here for four generations, even if some of those generations hadn't been as respectable as some might like. But no family was perfect.

His gaze swept across to the other hill, catching the last of the afternoon sun. If he stood on the seat of the ATV, he could catch a glint of the Darcy estate's solar farm, with the angled glass and metal absorbing radiant energy from the sun. Their ranch might be four times the size of the Reilly's, but the Darcy's greater focus on renewable energy in recent times had caused some furor among some of the other ranchers. Jackson could see the point of environmentally sustainable practices. And if he had spare dollars then he might investigate it more, too. But Reilly finances had never been flush; they kept the ranch afloat by sweat and prayers.

That thought led to another, and the memory of a certain woman's smile. Thank goodness his sister wasn't privy to everything Jackson thought, because ever since dropping Lexi home on Thursday night, he'd found himself wondering about her, caught between amazement about what she'd thought about him and Ellie, and anticipation about what Sunday would bring. Mucking out stalls, checking fence lines, struggling to get his head around finances, dealing with Mom ... none of it mattered. How could Lexi have thought he and Ellie were an item?

The fact she had, as Ellie had told him on their return from dropping Lexi off, had made him laugh so hard he'd almost missed the turnoff to their road.

"No wonder she was shy around you," Ellie had said. "I thought it was your natural unawesome charm, but apparently she sees something not one hundred percent unattractive. Weird. I don't understand it at all."

"Be weird if you did."

"So modest."

"That's me."

Her snort of laughter made him smile. But his sister's words had buoyed his heart. Okay, so it was nice to know he hadn't inadvertently done something to offend Ms. Franklin, and the fact she'd obviously tried to avoid him gladdened his heart. She might've misunderstood some things, but he liked that it stemmed from a deep respect for marriage vows, something his family hadn't exactly excelled in. Of course, Dermott and Mindy seemed to be chugging along fine, their visit for Christmas last year coming as a surprise. He'd never been close with his older brothers. Dermott had left when Jackson was ten, and Mitchell had been more focused on hockey than family.

Jackson had always been closer to Ellie and Cooper, even though they were both younger than him by several years. Cooper now worked in IT near San Jose. He wondered how old Lexi was …

The two-way radio crackled. "Jackson?" Denny Ronaldson, their ranch foreman called him. "It ain't good news. You better come to the barn real quick."

Jackson's heart clenched as he got on the ATV and accelerated up the hill. The barn beckoned, its traditional large red frame a badge of western movies everywhere, which was why it had proved a fun location for the town's New Year's Eve dance six months ago. Too bad those fun times had died not long after midnight.

Two minutes later he'd throttled down and switched off the ignition and raced inside. "Denny?"

"Over here," Denny called from the stall. Ellie stood nearby, arms crossed, forehead creased.

Jackson's heart sank some more as he drew near. He already knew what Denny was going to say, and he was right. It wasn't good at all. "It's Brutus, isn't it?"

"I don't think he's improved none."

Jackson gritted his teeth to stop an expletive from slipping out. Ever since that first bout of hot weather several weeks ago, Brutus had been out of sorts. He studied the bull, who seemed a far cry from the proud creature he'd paid top dollar for. "Do we call Jess in again?"

"I hate to say it, but I don't think that young filly knows a lot about bulls."

"I think you underestimate her," Ellie said. "She's savvier than people around here give her credit for."

"That remains to be seen," Denny muttered.

Jackson shot his sister a warning look—riling Denny wouldn't help—and they spent the next few minutes trying to soothe the bull whose kicking signaled an aggression he hoped wasn't a sign of inferior breeding. "I'm gonna call her anyway."

"Your dime." Denny spat on the ground, and walked back into the pen, crooning to the sick animal in a way that saw the old man keep his job when his ornery manners might've had him fired long ago.

"Jess is good," Ellie said. "She graduated top in her class."

"But Denny is right. She lacks experience."

"Which she won't get if nobody gives her a chance."

Jackson sighed. "Who else is there anyway?"

"James couldn't help having a heart attack."

Jess's dad had recently been forced into retirement. "Maybe he could come with her."

"He can't. He's on a cruise with his wife."

"Great. Well, call Jess. What's another call-out fee on top of everything else we already owe?"

Ellie bit her lip. "Are things that bad?"

Sometimes he hated having to tell the truth. "It's not as bad as it could be." Like, they weren't in such financial straits that they needed to sell the ranch. But if things didn't improve soon, that option yawned endlessly ahead of him. After spending years convincing his super-successful brothers that he was happy being the one stuck holding the reins of the ranch, so to speak, there was no way he was ever going to admit defeat. He had to make this work. And a big part of his vision for the future had been seeing Brutus fulfil his duty and become the stud for cows around here. But if the poor animal couldn't do the deed, then ...

He drew out his phone and moved outside to where phone reception worked better. There were dead pockets of phone coverage around here that not even the Darcy's millions had been able to improve.

After tapping some numbers, he got Martin's veterinary services. Their message bank, anyway. "Hey Jess, it's Jackson

Reilly. I'm afraid it's Brutus again. Can you please swing by as soon as you can? Thanks."

He rubbed his forehead. *God, I really need Your help. I don't see a way out of this mess. And I know You care more about people than animals, but could you please heal poor Brutus, too?*

CHAPTER FIVE

There was something beautiful and so relaxing about looking out over gently hilled farmland, as the roadside trees flashed past. Lexi's anticipation grew. She'd never spent much time on farms. She'd always been a city or at least a town girl, so her knowledge of animals and plants was limited to the thoroughly domesticated types. But here, looking out weathered hills of green undulating to blues and purples, it felt like she was in a painting. A place of peace, as far removed as possible from the emergency room of her nightmares.

She glanced across to where Jackson was driving, her insides knotting at her foolishness. How could she have assumed he and Ellie were anything but brother and sister? It seemed obvious now, but perhaps it had originated from a degree of defensiveness that led her to mistrust any handsome man. Something that had only happened when she realized how deadly some handsome men could be.

Jackson glanced across and smiled, but his smile didn't seem to hold the same light as it had earlier this week. At church this morning Ellie had mentioned something about Jackson being worried about a bull. Lexi had offered to stay home, but Ellie wouldn't hear of it.

"I've been looking forward to this all week. And we made a ton of food. And my mom is expecting you, so please don't let our troubles stop you from coming."

Troubles?

She recognized trouble in the pleat in Jackson's brow. The man was worried, and she found herself praying for peace.

He shifted in his seat and glanced at her again. "I hope you're a fan of potato salad."

"I love it," she said.

"Like hot dogs too?"

"Not as much." The brief unit she'd studied as part of the nutrition component of her nursing degree meant that she'd become less a fan of such highly processed foods. Not that she would admit to that.

"Just as well Jackson is cooking ribs today," Ellie said from behind.

"You cook?" she asked him.

"You don't?" he countered.

"I like to eat, so yes."

"Me too," he said, eyes fixed on the road.

"I just thought all ranches had cooks and staff who do that."

"Meet the cook." Ellie waved from the back seat.

"Not your mother?"

She noticed how Jackson exchanged a glance with Ellie in the rear vision mirror. "Mom isn't up to doing much these days."

"I'm sorry," Lexi murmured, wondering if she should press for more details. "Is she unwell?"

The silence greeting her question gave enough answer. As did the way Jackson's shoulders lifted slightly as he tensed. "Her health has declined quite a lot in recent years," he finally said.

"It's partly why I help out as much as I do," Ellie said. "Otherwise it'd be poor Jackson struggling all alone."

Lexi guessed from the way Jackson's jaw clenched, and the muscle throbbing in his jaw that he wasn't a huge fan of his sister's assessment. But it only made her more curious about this family. And the nurse inside couldn't help but wonder what Mrs. Reilly's health issue involved.

They passed a series of new-looking white fences that seemed to carry on for miles. "That's a big property," she said, gesturing to the side. "Is it yours?"

"It's the Darcy's," Jackson said.

"They're the really rich people around here. Out here, at least," Ellie said. "There's a bunch of people in town who think they're pretty special, but we don't pay as much attention to them. Liam is nice, but he's not here often. He's always travelling for work. Or in Seattle, seeing his girlfriend."

"They're in Africa now," Jackson said, almost absently.

"Africa?"

"Something about water wells in poor countries."

"Wow."

"Yeah. He's nice," Ellie said. "I don't know him too well, and his sister Georgia tends to keep to herself. But Jackson and Liam get on well."

So Jackson was friends with the richest man in these parts. That had to have its challenges.

He slowed the vehicle as they approached an entry that looked surprisingly grand. She'd guessed from the rust and dings in the panels that Jackson's truck wasn't new, and stories involving hardship didn't exactly lend themselves to expensive-looking stone-walled gates, nor fancy signs spelling out Reilly Ranch in scripted letters. "What a nice entrance."

"Yeah, that's Dermott's work. My oldest brother built it for Mom as a surprise for Mother's Day years ago." Another glance passed between the siblings. "Let's just say the gift was not received as well as Dermott had hoped."

"Oh."

"Yeah. He does gardening and landscaping work in the east, on the Independence Islands near South Carolina. We don't see him much. This past Christmas was the first time he'd been back in nearly twenty years."

"Families aren't always easy."

"That's for sure."

"You … you mentioned some other brothers as well." Lexi turned to look at Ellie. "Do they live here too?"

"Nope. Mitchell plays hockey in Minnesota, and Cooper is in Silicon Valley. They don't tend to come back here unless they have to."

Interesting. The more the siblings shared, the more curious she was about what she would find.

The driveway continued for half a mile until they came to a stand of pines. Beyond that lay a white homey-looking two-story house, with a red roof and door. Both looked like they needed repainting. An attempt to prettify the garden saw roses planted in orderly lines, blooming in pinks and reds and yellows. But the garden beds needed weeding, and the whole place had a slightly depressed air.

"Thanks again for inviting me," she said, forcing cheer to her voice.

"Thanks for coming," Ellie said as Jackson pulled to a stop and quit the engine.

She got out, narrowly missing a pile of horse manure. That sure would've been a great first impression for Mrs. Reilly.

She followed Ellie up the front steps, through the glass-paned front door into a dim timber-lined hall. Talk about ranch-like. Any second now and she'd see a hat-stand filled with Stetsons, maybe a cowhide on the floor, and—

A glance at the living room had her swallowing a chuckle. A

brown-and-white cowhide did indeed lie on the tiled floor between dark leather sofas. Her gaze drifted up the walls. One wall held a large photograph of the hills, which she guessed might've been taken nearby. "Is this from around here?"

"It's the ranch—well, most of it. Liam's sister, Georgia, took the picture."

"She's pretty talented."

"Yeah." Again there was that tone of resignation in Jackson's voice, almost like he wasn't the world's hugest fan of the Darcy family, even though Ellie had said he and Liam were friends.

"Something smells good," Lexi said, sniffing the air.

"Jackson has a special sauce. It's a secret. He won't even tell me." Ellie rolled her eyes.

"Like the Colonel's eleven secret herbs and spices?"

"You know that was just marketing, right?" Ellie said.

"Really?"

"Ah. So that's a no."

Lexi swapped grins with her, glad to have found someone she could almost regard as the sister she'd never had. Her brother, Matt, was ten years older, so Lexi had felt like an only child for much of her life. Of course, that had both advantages and disadvantages, chief of which was that Lexi had become the center of her mother's world. It had taken university studies on the opposite side of the planet to convince Mum that she could survive, something that had lasted through Lexi's first five years of work. Until she almost hadn't.

"Is your mother around?" she asked Ellie quietly.

"I'll go see."

Ellie disappeared down a narrow hallway and knocked on a door at the end. Not wanting to seem like she was spying, Lexi moved to the kitchen where Jackson was crouched down, looking through the glass door of the oven.

"Is there anything I can do?" she asked.

"You're a guest," he said. "Guests don't have to help."

"Well, I'm glad to know they don't *have* to help." She tried to inject a smile into her tone. "But what if they want to?"

He pushed upright, and she got a sense as to how tall he really was. The muscles in his arm said hard work was nothing new, and she caught a whiff of something that smelled like leather, moss, and something very male. Her stomach tensed, and she stepped back. Released a slow, appreciative breath.

There was a lot to appreciate about Jackson Reilly. His faith, his height, his breadth, his strength, his willingness to cook. Call her shallow, but some of these were qualities she'd come to value a lot more in recent months.

"Would you like a drink?"

"Yes, please." The warm weather and dry dusty conditions left her throat parched.

He poured her a glass of lemonade and she was gently directed to the table where she sat and was met a half minute later by an apologetic Ellie.

"Mom is sorry, but she's not feeling well today."

"Is there something I can help with?"

Ellie shot a look at Jackson then shook her head. "Mom is often tired, and she doesn't like to keep seeing doctors."

"Lots of people don't." But they were often the very people who needed medical attention. Perhaps she might be able to help another way, another day.

The next twenty minutes flew past in a flurry of plates, food, and laughter. Lexi hadn't expected to enjoy herself this much, but the teasing between brother and sister warmed her heart, reminding her of the ease which she used to find with friends from church, or her colleagues in her nursing unit. Comfortable, with easy rapport, questions flinging back and forth.

"So, nursing. Did you have a specialty?" Jackson asked, taking a sip of his cola.

"I'd wondered about pediatrics, but maybe I'm a wuss, I just couldn't be brave enough when the really sick kids came in."

"That would be hard." His dark eyes softened with compassion.

She nodded, her throat thickening. "I'm not great at telling people their child is dying."

"I don't think many people would be."

She studied the faded floral print of the dinner plate. "I ended up doing a stint in emergency, when—" Why was she saying this? Her hand reached up and adjusted the scarf at her throat. Maybe she was extra self-conscious today, but it seemed people at church had been looking at her more closely. Maybe her scarf had slipped the other day and revealed something of her trauma to the world.

"When what?" Ellie asked.

"Sorry." She shook her head. "I … had a bad accident at work, it's not something I like to talk about much." Or ever.

"Fair enough." Jackson's lips curved.

She ducked her head, even though his smile had a way of easing the jagged corner of her heart. He might have some challenges of his own, but there was something soothing about this man, something her heart responded to. And his long-lashed dark eyes and curly hair only added to his appeal.

"Let's clean up, then we'll give you a tour of the ranch." Ellie pushed her seat out, then paused. "Actually, how about I clean up while you two start that tour?"

"I can help," Lexi said.

"I'm sure you can, but I'm also pretty sure you heard Jackson before. We don't let guests help. And seeing Jackson did the cooking, I'm on cleaning detail. Alas." But her grin suggested she was not unhappy at all.

"You'd better excuse my sister," Jackson said, with a fond glance at Ellie. "She gets ideas into her head and runs off with them like she's in a marathon. It can take days before she's willing to hear sense."

"One of the excitable ones, huh?"

"Exactly."

Lexi pushed back her chair. "Do I need boots and a hat to check out the ranch?"

"Only if you're planning on moving here full-time," Ellie said.

Lexi swallowed. Why did that sound like an invitation?

Jackson slid open the glass door to outside, then they were on a concrete terrace that led to the fenced backyard. Beyond lay a huge red barn, like something she'd seen in the movies, complete with hitching rails and water troughs for horses. A dog ran up to her, barking and sniffing around her, and she shifted uneasily.

"Hey, it's okay," Jackson said. "This is Fido."

"Fido? Seriously?"

"We don't tend to do creativity around here." Jackson shrugged. "Hey, girl, behave."

Excuse me?

Oh. The way he drew a hand through the dog's fur indicated he was talking to the dog.

"This is Lexi. She's a friend. Be nice." He glanced up at her again. "Put your hand down, let her sniff you."

She obeyed, and the dog sniffed then licked her hand. "Hello, Fido." She glanced at Jackson. "I always thought Fido was a boy's name."

"Really? They call boys Fido in Australia?"

She wrinkled her nose at him, and he laughed. She had to admit liking the sound of that deep rumble. Like his smile, his chuckle had a way of making her feel secure.

He pushed upright again and drew Fido's attention with a click of his fingers. "Come on, girl. Let's show our guest what we do here."

———

JACKSON STOLE a glance at Lexi as she sat on the wooden fence, studying the land like she was prepping for an exam. He wasn't sure if she was impressed. She'd been in a state of oohs and ahhs over the view—ten points in her favor—but she also had a way of making him feel off-center, like he was riding lopsided and about to tumble off any second. Maybe he was bad at reading women's signals. Or maybe Lexi's signals were so mixed he couldn't tell which was which. All he knew was that the shy, nervy woman of last Sunday seemed to have disappeared sometime during the week, and the woman sitting next to him seemed to own more confidence than he'd originally thought.

But it was kind of nice to be able to point out some of the improvements he'd made, such as the new pens and dams, things his grandfather had wanted to do but hadn't. After their father had left when Ellie was a baby, it had seemed impossible to get the ranch to a standard deemed acceptable. Looking at the improvements now drew his spine straighter.

"So you have cows?" she asked.

"Beef cattle, yeah." He pointed out several dozen amber-colored beasts in the homestead paddock. "Red Angus, to be precise."

"Like the steak?"

"Yes, ma'am." He grinned at her wrinkled nose.

"I thought Angus cattle were black."

"Red Angus is a newer breed. The meat is a little sweeter and fattier, so restaurants are willing to pay top dollar for it."

She nodded, biting her lip as if she couldn't believe the animals would be eaten one day. But that's what they did here. From gate to plate. And if Brutus was ever to start doing his business, then he'd have a new line—from conception to consumption. But maybe now wasn't the time to focus on that. "We also have sheep, chickens, and horses."

"A real farm."

Ranch, but whatever.

"That must've been fun growing up."

"Yeah." That was the short answer. Long answer was that ranching was a lot of hard work. Constant hard work, especially for his mom. Maybe there was a reason his brothers had all left.

A faint howl echoed across the valley. She shivered and moved a little closer to him. "Call me crazy, but that sounded like a wolf."

"You're not crazy."

"It was? You get wolves around here?"

"Occasionally. We see more coyotes."

Her eyes widened behind her sunglasses. "I thought wolves were extinct."

"They almost were, but they've been reintroduced. There are several packs across east Washington. We sometimes hear them at night."

She rubbed her upper arms. "Aren't they a threat to your animals?"

He shrugged, his lips tweaking wryly. "It's still illegal to hunt them."

"So what can you do?"

"Electric fencing. Making sure our fences are maintained."

"Electric fencing must be expensive." Her brow knit, like she cared.

"Yeah. We combine it with turbo-fladry, which they're reluctant to cross, so they get conditioned to staying away."

"What's turbo-fladry?"

"It's a string of red or orange cloth flags hung at eighteen-inch intervals along a fence."

"That works?"

"Seems to so far. We also sometimes use fox lights, which simulate a flashlight moving around." One of the coolest inventions he'd come across. "But our best method of protection involves riding the boundaries, checking on the stock, making sure there's nothing to attract them. Wolves are scavengers. If they get a whiff of a dead carcass, they'll hunt for more. So we have to be careful." He'd once seen a pit where wily wolves had dug through several feet of dirt to ravage the remains of a dead bull. It hadn't been pretty.

She shivered. "Have you ever been attacked?"

"No. And it's unlikely. They don't tend to attack humans."

"But sometimes they do. We see it in the news."

He shrugged. "The advice is the same as for bears. Stand up tall, use a big voice, and back away slowly."

"I hope I don't ever come across a wolf."

"You're unlikely to, especially living so near town. And even less likely when you go back to Australia."

What were her future plans? Did she hope to stay?

"I'm not sure when that will be, especially with my family being here."

"What about work?"

Her gaze slid away and he remembered what she'd said before. An accident. His chest tensed. Did that have anything to do with the scar on her neck?

His mind spun with a dozen possibilities of what could've caused such a thing. Surgery gone wrong? Maybe she'd run into a wire. He studied her as she looked away, wishing he could peer beneath the wispy gauzy fabric of her scarf and see what she was trying to hide.

As if sensing his interest, she put her hands on her hips and slowly pivoted away from him, taking in the long views over the range. "It's beautiful here."

His heart softened at her praise. "We're fans."

"Do you ever take in guests?"

Guests? "We don't really do sleepovers."

"I meant paying guests." She pointed to the bunkhouse next to the barn. "Is that accommodation?"

"For the workers." Although it had been built when they could afford more hands. Two thirds of the bunkhouse sat empty for most of the year. But tourists? Staying here? Green-horns getting where they shouldn't? No thanks. Reilly's was a working ranch, not a dude ranch. The thought of strangers poking around drew a shudder.

"Are you two done yet?"

Jackson turned to see Ellie approach. She tilted her head to Lexi and raised her brows, then threw a smile on her dial as Lexi moved to face her too.

"How are you doing, Lexi? Has he taken you inside the barn yet?"

"Not yet."

"Then it must be my turn to show you around."

Ellie drew them closer to the barn. Jose and Felipe weren't around—their horses were missing, so they were probably riding the boundary again. Denny was likely having a smoke behind the bunkhouse, which was about as private as their workers could get. With Sunday being a go-slow day on the ranch—as much as any ranch could have a day of rest—it wasn't surprising to find the place quieter than during the week.

"Lexi, do you know how to ride?" Ellie asked.

"No."

"Really?" Ellie's glance flicked back to Jackson, and there was no mistaking the intention in those baby blues. "Jackson might have to show you. I remembered something I need to do."

"Ellie," he warned.

"Sure you do." Lexi's crossed arms said she was buying none of it. "You just said it was your turn to show me around."

His spirits dipped. Didn't Lexi want to hang with him? He scuffed his boot in the dirt. See? This was a dumb idea. Anyway, she was returning home, and probably wouldn't want to spend a second longer—

"I don't mind being taught to ride." Lexi turned towards Jackson. "But only if someone doesn't feel pressured into doing so."

"Hear that, Jackson?" Ellie said. "I think Lexi is saying she's happy for you to teach her to ride."

"Got it loud and clear, sister dear." He lifted his gaze to fuse with Lexi's. Her lips were curved in a half smile, and the camaraderie he saw in her expression brought ease to his soul. "I'd be real happy to teach Ms. Franklin to ride, but a dress and sandals won't cut it."

"In other words, you'll need to come back one day soon," Ellie said with a bright smile.

"If I'm to learn to ride, yes." Lexi's smile lifted to catch him around the heart.

Oh, he'd be willing to teach her. Especially if it meant he could learn more about this intriguing woman.

"Or you could come and hang out." Ellie was obviously determined to get her poor brother a date. "You know, like, eat a meal together, watch the stars, maybe—"

"Thanks, Ellie. I don't think we need any more of your suggestions," Jackson said.

"You're sure? Because I have plenty."

"I bet you do." Lexi met his gaze with a hint of conspiracy. "So do I get to see inside the barn, or is someone going to take me home?"

"Ooh, bossy." Ellie nudged him in the side. "I like it."

Lexi eyed Ellie as though she didn't know what to make of her. Which made two of them.

"Lexi, would you like to look inside the barn?" Jackson asked. "We've got some stables at the back, and some pens we use when—"

Oh. That's right. Brutus. He glanced at his watch. Had time slipped away that much? Jess Martin was due to arrive this afternoon, having declared the other day that she couldn't yet determine what was wrong. She'd said she might know in a few days.

Those few days were now, so he'd have to forgo driving Lexi

home. This didn't sit well, especially when he now felt the urge to apologize for his sister's blatant manipulations.

Maybe a quick tour of the barn would work. He directed her through on the Cliff's Notes edition, pointing out things of interest, which didn't take long. He figured a nurse's interest levels would be way less than a rancher's.

"Jackson turned this into a dance hall for New Year's," his ever-helpful sister said. "It looked amazing, with twinkling lights everywhere. It seemed like half the town was here."

"Sounds fun."

"Look at my photos."

It seemed to take an age for the pictures on Ellie's phone to be looked at and exclaimed over, and Jackson grew increasingly aware of the time. "We should probably get you home soon," he said, when it seemed Lexi had seen every last one of Ellie's photos.

"Sure."

But when they went out the front it was to see a bright red Dodge pickup pulling in, dust lifting behind. "Hey, Jackson, Ellie," Jess Martin said, lifting a hand. "I came to see how Brutus is. Hope you don't mind that I'm a little early. I meant to tell you at church but got called out to a calving gone wrong late last night and slept in. But anyway, I'm here now." She seemed to notice Lexi. "Hey. Jess Martin, veterinarian."

"Lexi Franklin." Lexi offered a smile.

"She's the daughter of Peter Franklin, from the Bible school in town," Ellie said.

"Pleased to meet you." Jess grinned at Lexi then turned to Jackson. "Are you ready to show me how Brutus is getting on?"

He nodded, pivoting to Lexi. "Thanks for coming."

"Thanks for having me."

"Um …" He scratched the back of his neck. "I was wondering if maybe you might like—"

"Hey, Jackson, you mind if I just go down to the barn?" Jess said.

"Sure. I'll be there in a sec." He focused on Lexi, doing his best to ignore his sister and her mile-wide smirk. She sauntered off to his car. Typical. She'd insist on driving his vehicle, not hers, and he could bet a million dollars she wouldn't put gas in it. He shook his head.

Lexi's brow now wore a crease. "You should probably see to your … Brutus, was it?"

"My bull. He's not doing well. We'd hoped he'd be a stud, but he's firing blanks."

She blinked. "Right. Well …"

Look at him making small talk, charming the lady with talk of his bull's infertility issues. Man. He wished he could be smooth like Liam Darcy. "See you around, Lexi."

She nodded. "See you around."

Then she turned and walked away.

CHAPTER SIX

"I don't know what to think anymore."

Lexi's footsteps stilled. Judging from the hushed murmurs coming from the living room, her parents were having a Serious Discussion. She had no wish to interrupt.

"—she's been a shadow of herself since the attack."

Breath suspended. They were talking about her?

"It's good she's finally making an effort and trying to fit in, but it's like that man took away our beautiful girl and left us with this pale imitation."

Lexi took a step back. Her mother's comment wasn't unfair. But it didn't mean Lexi liked to hear it.

"What should we do?"

Her father replied in a low-voiced mumble. She heard words like "pray" and "God's timing" and "friends" but anything more was too difficult to make out. And maybe that was for the best, because eavesdroppers never heard good of themselves, did they?

She took another step back, and the wooden floor squeaked.

"Lexi? Is that you?"

Caught. Pretend she hadn't heard, or go in with guns blazing? She made a face at herself—look at her with the Western metaphors. Must be the effect of hanging out with a real-life cowboy.

"Hi." Aim for bright and breezy. Mum mightn't be far off the mark, but there was no need to make her any more worried than she needed to be. "What are you two talking about?"

Boom. Hit them with the truth question.

"You, actually," her father replied.

"How was your time at the ranch?" her mother asked.

"It was nice. Jackson made ribs, which were really tasty. They gave me a quick tour. It was fun."

Why did her mother's eyes seem to spark when Jackson's name was mentioned? For that matter, why did Lexi's cheeks feel hot when she mentioned his name? It wasn't like there was anything there, even with the sorta-flirty comments about him teaching her to ride. He hadn't meant it, obviously, because he hadn't arranged another day. And anyway, she wasn't looking for a man. She was here to recover from a trauma, not make plans for the rest of her life. Even if she did think Jackson was attractive.

"Ellie is a ball of energy, isn't she?" Mum said. "From what I understand she'd love to reopen the town museum, but ranch work keeps her busy."

"I didn't know that."

"There's a lot that family keeps to themselves," her father said.

Was that disapproval in her father's tone? Judging from the way her mother looked at Dad, Lexi wasn't the only one who had heard it. "Is there something you're trying to say, Dad?"

"Just be careful. You don't want to get too attached to people if you're planning to go back to Australia."

A chuckle escaped. "What, like you?"

"Of course not us," her father said. "We're your family."

"Exactly. So why can't I make friends with people, even if

one day I move back? I can stay in touch with my friends." She emphasized that last word a little, just to stop them getting ideas. "The same as I do with you."

"Of course you can." Mum shot Dad a look. "But if you are thinking at all about staying—not saying that you should, but you know I'd simply *love* for you to live nearer—"

Way to go with the no-guilt policy.

"—then you might want to consider what your future would be like here."

"You mean like getting qualified to nurse here?" Lexi asked. Subtlety had never been her strength.

"Or something like nursing. You have always had such deep compassion for people, and it would be a shame to see that wasted."

"I don't plan to waste it," Lexi said. "I just need more time."

More time, and more assurance that she'd never face that same level of threat again.

"Do you still feel scared?" her mother asked softly.

"I still don't like people moving behind me, if that's what you mean." As for medications, she was extremely wary about anyone who might be on drugs.

"Have you had any more correspondence from the hospital?"

"I told you about the last email. I haven't heard anything since."

"I'm sure they want you back," Dad reassured.

But Lexi was equally sure she didn't want to return.

Whoa. She stilled as the truth resounded in her spirit, like a gong in her soul bringing fresh awareness.

"Let us know when you make a decision, okay?" Mum said.

Lexi nodded, not trusting herself to speak. Especially not when this revelation was so new. She needed to think about it a little more, knead it in her mind, pull out the possibilities about how the shape of her future could look.

She slowly made her way up the creaky stairs to the room

she'd claimed as her own. This section of the house was like a private wing, complete with its own bathroom. It was separate from her parents' rooms—they had a kitchenette and living area as well as their own bedroom and ensuite bathroom—and separate from the dormitories where the students stayed. Whoever had designed this house seemed to have added a variety of rooms higgledy-piggledy, but they knew how to capitalize on the view. Her window looked out toward boats sailing on the blue shimmer of Lake Wainscott, the largest of the three lakes that gave the town its name. It was a perfect summer afternoon for someone to be down on the lake with their friends, making the most of the sunshine. And while she felt she might finally have made friends with Ellie and Jackson, her parents' caution about the family drew hesitation. She'd always trusted them, for both their godly wisdom and practical guidance. But this felt different, maybe a little—dare she admit it—judgmental. Or was it judgy to even admit that?

"Lord." She settled at the window seat, looking up at the gentle hills. "Help me to see clearly, and not through the lens of the past or through the prejudice or preconceptions of others."

A Psalm ticked into memory. "I lift my eyes to the hills, where does my help come from? My help comes from the Lord, the maker of heaven and earth."

She drew in a deep breath of sun-warmed air and let the verse settle into her spirit. The Lord was faithful, had proved himself faithful so often, especially over the past few months. She could've died, but God had saved her. She could've bled out, but the cut hadn't severed anything major. She could've lost her voice, but God had protected her. Apart from the scars on her skin and in her mind, she was practically the same as before.

Except maybe not. At least not according to her mother.

She moved to her laptop and found the email the hospital board had sent her, along with a promise of compensation. She hadn't wanted a lengthy court case and had been willing to settle out of court, but the nurse's union representative had begged her to be the figurehead of a campaign for better nurse safety. If her actions could protect another nurse from going through what she had, well, wasn't that worth doing?

A bird's call drew her gaze outside, and her mind flicked to the promise of God's word. God was her helper, her protector, her strong tower. While trusting in people might prove fallible, trusting in God would always see her safe. Not that it would mean she would never see trouble, but at least she knew she wasn't alone.

She touched her throat, thanking God for the thousandth time that He'd protected her. That He'd proved himself strong on her behalf.

But she never wanted to be put in that situation again. Never wanted to feel that fear, feel that pain, feel her life slipping away, pooling on the floor in a sticky, bloody mess.

Another glance at the email, and she flagged it to check on later, then tapped open the tab she'd saved from her restless Googling yesterday.

Transferring qualifications for nurses in Washington state.

JACKSON EXHALED SLOWLY, pressing his fingers deep into his forehead. Jess's latest tests confirmed the first batch. Brutus seemed to be sterile, and all Jackson's hopes were shot.

He'd have to email the ranches he'd set up for Brutus's stud work and let them know. He'd have to decide whether to keep the bull or send him to the slaughterhouse. He'd have to find another way to fund the ranch expenses, to generate the income they so desperately needed.

"God, what do I do?" His voice cracked as he prayed. Thank God Ellie wasn't here to see her big brother so close to breaking. "Show me what to do, please Lord."

An internal nudge throbbed, like a splinter swallowed into skin. He'd noticed it ever since Sunday, a prodding that lay just beyond his consciousness. Whether it was the devastating news about Brutus or general busyness, he didn't know. It remained hard to grasp, buried under layers of fears. But he didn't have time to chase it down now.

His phone bleeped a message and panic rose again. An automated "kind" reminder of the vet bill payment that remained outstanding.

Outstanding it certainly wasn't. Unless it was another outstanding testimony to his utter stupidity. He pushed the thought to one side, and concentrated on writing to those he'd promised Brutus's stud services. Perhaps it wasn't too late in the season for them to make other arrangements.

He sent the emails off, then squinted at the wages. Thank God his workers were few, so that it hadn't reached a point yet when it was a choice between paying them or paying the electricity—

A ping alerted him to an incoming email. He glanced at it, his spirits sinking as he read the terse reply to his apology about Brutus. Words like "incompetent" and "inadequate" and "second-rate" sure made a guy feel good. But he couldn't blame them. He felt the same way.

He switched off email notifications—who needed more discouraging interruptions to their day?—and tried to wrap his brain around the orders for feed and forage. Thank God for Denny, who could keep eyes on the animals. He was deep into wrestling numbers when a knock preceded an opening door.

"Jackson?"

Irritation spiked as he pushed back from the computer, rubbing his eyes to ease the strain. He'd been staring at way too many computer screens lately. He glanced at the door where Ellie stood, her brow knit. "What's up now?"

He tried to temper the edge in his voice by gritting out a

smile. But there'd been too many interruptions this week, too many thoughts spiraling out of control, just like their finances. Maybe he'd have to beg the bank for a new loan. On his hands and knees if necessary. Because if he'd done his sums right, they were in the red so much it was like watching his life bleed out.

"Have you seen Mom?"

"Nope." His mother never came into the office that had once been her bedroom. When her husband had left—none of them had called that man their father in years—she'd revamped the sleeping arrangements and stuck the oldest two boys in here while she'd claimed Dermott's old room at the opposite end of the house. Later, when Dermott and Mitchell had left, this room had become a living space until Cooper left and Jackson's responsibilities meant he'd repurposed it as the office. "Why?"

"She's missing again."

"Again?" He arched a brow.

"I don't know what's going on." His sister moved past teetering stacks of files he needed to sort out but had put off until a rainy day. Trouble was, rainy days required focus on other things. "She's gotten so vague, I don't even think she recognizes me some days."

"What?" His world felt like a pack of cards tumbling down in space.

"Surely you've noticed it too."

No. Truth be told, he'd barely spoken to his mother in what felt like weeks. Remorse stung, swearing louder than any blue-worded email from disappointed fellow ranchers.

"So you don't know where she is?"

"No." She gestured to his two-way radio, lying half-buried under another pile of bank statements. "Can you call the guys, see if anyone's seen her?"

"Sure." He snatched it up, rose, and followed his sister as she made a quick pass of all the rooms. His chest tensed. Okay, so this was concerning. He stabbed the button that would alert Denny and all hands. "Anyone seen my mom?"

He winced at how that sounded, like a lost little boy. But that was how he felt most days. Lost. Drowning in a sea of paperwork, debt, and fears.

The walkie-talkie crackled. "No boss."

"No, sir."

"Nope."

"Sorry."

"Lo siento."

"Keep an eye out for her and let me know."

There came a bunch of affirmations and he shoved the radio in his pocket, his gut clenching.

"So where is she?" He veered to the bunkhouses as Ellie hurried to the barn. With over 250 acres of land, someone could easily lose their way if they strayed too far. And while he'd tried to assure Lexi that wolves didn't attack humans, he didn't want to take chances with Mom. Especially as she was looking kind of frail these days.

"Mom? Are you in here?" He pushed open the door to one of the old bunkhouse rooms.

It was dark, the musty scent and dust that flew as he flicked on the light suggesting no one had been here for months. Still, it was worth checking. He peered into the furthest corner, even checked under the bottom bunks. No luck.

He closed the door and did the same in the next two rooms as well. Still nothing. Where was she?

Another room, this one occupied by Felipe. He moved to open the door, feeling a little funny checking here without them, when the walkie-talkie crackled again.

"I got her." Denny.

"Where are you?"

"Down near the machinery shed."

The machinery shed? What was she doing there? "I'll be right there."

He yelled for Ellie and hurried to the shed, positioned halfway down the hill from the barn. He could see Denny holding something that looked like a checked blanket around his mom's shoulders. What the—?

"Mom?" As he drew closer, he could see why.

His mother was dressed in a white nightgown, her bare feet covered in mud, her hair string-like and looking grayer than ever.

"Mom?" Jackson drew close, nodding to Denny who shot him a look he couldn't interpret before moving away. Jackson wrapped an arm around her. "Mom, are you okay?"

She looked at him, and for a second, he could see the woman she'd once been—sad but courageous, exhausted but doing all she could to keep her kids clothed and fed.

"Donald?"

He blinked, a shudder curling up his back at that name. "Mom, I'm Jackson."

She peered at him, her faded blue eyes remaining dull, without recognition. "Who?"

"I'm your son. Jackson."

"Who?" She shook her head and pulled away. "I don't have a son."

His breath hitched, and he watched blankly as Ellie drew close and secured the blanket more firmly around his mother's shoulders.

She didn't recognize him. She'd mistaken him for the person he loathed more than any other. Nausea rippled through his stomach.

He watched for a moment as Ellie escorted her back up the hill, breath escaping in a heavy exhale as he scrubbed his fingers into his scalp.

A cleared throat nearby drew his attention to Denny.

"Thanks so much."

"She doesn't look well." His foreman stated the obvious.

"No." Now he was paying attention, he could see his mother looked more frail than his dim memories of his grandmother. When had this happened? Why hadn't he noticed? A glance around the rusting machinery reminded him of the reason why. "I need to call the doctor."

Denny made a non-committal sound, but Jackson didn't have time to chase that now. He didn't have time for much at all.

With long strides he hurried back to the house, in time to hear Ellie croon about washing Mom's feet and getting her settled in bed again. His throat thickened. When had this happened? Why hadn't he realized how bad she was?

He moved to the kitchen and switched on the coffee maker. Mom had always liked her coffee. Maybe they still had a pack of those windmill cookies she'd always liked. Little reminders of such things might provide enough comfort to help her snap back to the present. But try as he might, hunting through the cupboards and pantry revealed no pack of cookies, only a stale container of wafer biscuits he figured even Fido would turn her nose up at.

"What are you doing?" Ellie asked.

"Looking for windmill cookies."

Her eyes softened like she knew why. "We haven't had any in years."

Of course they hadn't. "What's wrong with her?"

"I don't know. I've never seen her this bad before. She's never wandered off like that either."

"She called me Donald."

The face she made matched the turmoil in his gut. "Ugh."

"She hasn't seen him in over twenty years. Why would she do that?"

"Maybe she thinks you look like him."

Perish the thought. Anyway, he wouldn't know. All memories of that man had been expunged over the years. It was almost as if Donald Reilly hadn't existed, save for the DNA running through five people's veins.

He finished doctoring the coffee just the way Mom preferred, and together they returned to the bedroom. He tapped on the door, even though it was open. The room was dim, but he could see her lying in bed, her fingers restless against the covers.

"Mom, here's your coffee," he said, placing it on top of the bedside table.

She nodded but said nothing, her gaze fixed on the sliver of light where the curtains didn't quite meet.

"Mom? Are you feeling okay?"

What a stupid question. How could she be? Where had the energetic woman of his youth gone? When had his memories overtaken what could be clearly seen?

A tug on his arm saw Ellie draw him back outside, her gaze sober.

"I didn't know she had got so bad."

She sighed, nodding, her mouth a flat line. "You know what this means?"

"I'm gonna call the doctor immediately."

Another nod. "Besides that."

The look she sent him drew the strings of his heart into a new kind of tense.

"You're gonna have to call the brothers."

He closed his eyes, tension rippling through what felt like every one of his pores. As Ellie promised to call the doctor and keep an eye on Mom, he headed back to the office and thumbed through the apps on his phone until he found the app he and his siblings used when they wanted to communicate. The last message had been two months ago. Yeah, they were that close. He slowly tapped out the message.

Hey. We need to talk ASAP. Something's wrong with Mom.

CHAPTER SEVEN

I t was quite possible she might be a little bit in love.

After a morning spent helping her mom make scones to be reheated for next week's summer visitors, Lexi had been released to spend a few hours in Trinity Lakes. It was nice to escape the unspoken questions of her parents and all the drama and pressure her new decision seemed to demand. Especially when it meant she got to visit places like this.

She smiled at the display of vintage teacups, all set out as if readying for a *Downton Abbey*-like high tea. The antique vibe was further reinforced by several porcelain dolls and teddy bears dressed up as if ready to partake. It was so unexpectedly enchanting, so whimsical, and yet another surprising addition to the charm of Trinity Lakes.

She'd stumbled into the Village Shoppes Emporium down an alley off Main Street while trying to escape a couple of people she'd thought she recognized from last week's pool party. She must've entered via the side entrance, as the barn-like building seemed to have been a former hardware store, judging from some of the signage and paraphernalia decorating the wooden beams and ceiling. But the floor space had been transformed into a series of cubbyhole-type stores, decorated like an old western town, with murals and painted props suggesting an old church, a barbershop, a school, and more. Each stall showcased different products to sell—candles, handcrafted toys and jewelry, vintage books, furniture, recycled fashion.

The space reminded her of local markets she used to enjoy visiting on Saturdays, except here everything was under cover. While few of the stalls had a shopkeeper, it seemed the price-tag system meant you could take things to a centralized counter and purchase your items there.

So far, she'd spied a pair of earrings she thought her mother might like for her birthday, and tried on a vintage leather jacket that might fit Lexi's own retro glamor vibe. She fingered a soft-as-silk scarf, wondering if she could justify the cost. Maybe she could, considering the last scarf had been all but destroyed after its chlorinated adventures last week.

She finished the last of the complimentary honey stick the kind man at the counter had offered and threw the plastic wrapper into the trash can near the café. Another place she might have to check out, judging from the delectable smells.

After purchasing the scarf and earrings—she'd need to think about the jacket, considering it wasn't exactly cold, and she'd always believed if something remained until she returned it was meant to be hers, but if not, c'est la vie—she exited, blinking against the afternoon sun. Heat rose through the pavement. Maybe she should've bought an ice-cream after all.

She moved across the street and was about to claim a seat under a shady looking tree when a black pickup drove past.

She recognized it. She'd traveled in it just last Sunday. She pivoted to watch it travel past, then pull in and park, the driver staying seated for a long moment.

Maybe he was checking his phone. Maybe he was—oh, nope. He was getting out. Moving to the green-roofed bank, straightening his shoulders as he clutched a packet of papers.

He pulled open the glass doors and disappeared into the yawning darkness. Okay, she'd spent a little too much time thinking about him in recent days. She'd be far better off thinking about what to do with the rest of her life.

She shifted on the wooden seat, the scent of summer holding a different scent to what she remembered from home. But while there might not be any sea-salt tang here, Trinity Lakes had a lovely essence of its own. She'd sensed it in the Village Shoppes, the way the community trusted each other and its visitors to not steal. She'd seen it last week, in the aftermath of the near-drowning, when all Barb's visitors had pitched in to help clean up without being asked, while Lexi had sat working to regain her composure. She'd experienced it in the friendly vibes as she moved around town, the sense that people genuinely liked each other. Maybe it was a bigger city thing, but she was used to people building walls, not bridges, focusing on themselves, not others, keeping to themselves, aloof, mistrustful of motives. It didn't seem like people did standoffishness here. Maybe that was a small-town thing.

She could see why her parents loved living in Trinity Lakes. Maybe she could settle here too. Unease roiled through her stomach as the web searches she'd undertaken recently rolled through her mind. Transferring her qualifications meant far more than simply filling out a couple of forms. It meant several rounds of applications, international university transcript validation, sitting yet another exam, background checks, and more. And while she didn't dispute any of that, the fact it would take far longer—and cost more—than she'd imagined, made moving back to Australia more appealing. Or at least exploring an alternative career path.

But the thought of giving up all she'd worked so hard for over many years still felt like another victory to the man who had already stolen so much. Why should she lose her career due to his actions?

"Lord." The micro-prayer might be one word, but she knew God heard her heart.

She closed her eyes, glad for the sunglasses that hid her eyes, which might stop any passersby from wondering if she was a town drunk sitting talking to herself in the park.

A bird's persistent twittering drew her attention above, and then her gaze fell on the bank across the street. This was stupid. She rose from her position. She had no wish to give off stalker vibes and make a certain somebody think she was watching him.

She was halfway to her car when the bank's doors opened and Jackson reappeared.

Oh. She swallowed and stumbled to a stop.

Okay, so she had thought Jackson Reilly looked good dressed in jeans, boots, and a checked shirt. But that was nothing compared to seeing him dressed up. Sure, the jeans and boots might be much the same, although a little less faded and scuffed, but with a nice collared shirt and jacket, and his usual spray of whiskers freshly shaved, it wasn't surprising that her heart double thumped.

But he looked grave, his frowning gaze to the ground, his posture holding a weary droop, like what he'd just experienced had snuffed the hope from him. Should she bother him? Maybe he'd prefer to be alone. That'd probably be best. And if she stayed quiet, he'd likely not see her …

"Jackson," she called, like her mouth was unattached to her brain.

His gaze lifted to meet hers and he stopped, then seemed to waver. For a dreadful second, she thought he might hurry away. Then he seemed to make up his mind and draw closer, pushing his grim face into a smile. "Hey, Lexi."

"Hi." She smiled. The way he looked at her, all serious and deep, seemed to steal sense from her brain. Quick, think of more conversation. "You're looking rather dashing." She winced. Dashing? Seriously? Maybe the *Downton Abbey* vibes from earlier had got stuck into her brain.

His lips curled up a little more. "That's me. Dashing from here to there."

"Busy, busy, busy, huh?"

"You know it."

Actually she didn't know it. Apart from cleaning and cooking at the college, her days stretched rather too long. Long enough to chase down rabbit trails about her future, and imaginings that probably weren't helpful for her mental health. It was a far cry from those days when she'd never had enough time to squeeze in work, church commitments, friends, and the gym.

"Are you too busy for a coffee?" Where had those words come from? "I mean, it would be nice to catch up. But only if you have time."

He studied her a moment, glanced at the pavement, then back up again. And the expression in his eyes—something like bleakness—suggested she not let him go until she knew for sure that he was okay.

"Please?"

She'd never begged a man before. Not to have coffee with her anyway. But a weird kind of stubbornness wouldn't let go, probably that same stubbornness that insisted she would not die, even as blood had spilled around the hands clutched at her throat.

"Sure," he finally said. "I don't know how much time I have, but coffee sounds great."

———

Sipping a latte in the diner where everyone knew each other's business when all he wanted to do was hide was not exactly his idea of fun. But when a beautiful woman stops a hurting man in the street and her pleading eyes practically force him to have coffee with her, well, what could a decent guy do but say yes?

Although now, sitting in the plastic booth next to the window for all the town to see, he'd give anything to be somewhere else. Even if there was nobody he'd rather be with.

He studied Lexi, her head bent as she tackled the last few bites of her peach pie. Her fluster at the many types of pie had lightened his anguish for a few moments at least, as she wrestled between trying the cherry, apple, huckleberry, and peach. "I mean, I'm always a sucker for a good apple pie, but I can't remember the last time I had peach. And then, I feel like I should be having huckleberry as a kind of patriotic thing." She'd tilted her head to one side. "What would you recommend?"

"You can always come back and try another some other time."

"True." The furrow between her eyes eased as she'd smiled up at Marlene. "Guess that means I'm having the peach."

"Ice cream and cream?"

"Why not?" Lexi turned to him. "You sure you can't be tempted?"

He'd shaken his head, knowing just how close to temptation he really was.

He was tempted to give up. Tempted to pack it all in. Tempted to rob a bank. Well, the last, not really. Not at *all*. But God felt far away, and the crushing weight of his problems was grinding him down.

She continued her chatter, telling him about some village shopping place nearby with all kinds of little stores. He half-listened, her conversation like a cool balm on the sting of disappointment after his encounter with Millie. What would he say to his brothers? His brothers, who'd likely insist Mom get seen by specialists, and he be forced to explain he couldn't afford it?

What did any of them know about struggling for money? Mitchell certainly didn't, not with his high-paying NHL career.

Dermott might've, once upon a time, but he was probably rolling in cash now he had his own business, Greener Gardens. And Cooper wouldn't have a clue either. He was all fancy cars and the latest tech toys. Nope. None of them had a clue. And he sure as heck wasn't going to go putting out his hand and asking for their help to keep the ranch afloat. Then they'd know for sure that his attempts to run the ranch had been exactly that. An attempt. In which he'd failed.

"Want to try some pie?" Lexi said now. "It's really good."

"Thanks, but I'm fine."

She nodded, as if she didn't really believe that last comment.

So far, he'd managed to avoid her questions about what he was doing in town, simply saying it was a business thing. Bless her. She hadn't pressed for more details, simply eyeing him in that way she had, like she could see beneath the surface of his skin to the scared little boy hiding within. His grip tightened on the coffee mug, so tight, tighter—and then the handle snapped, spilling dark brown liquid all over the table, all the way across into her lap.

"Oh shoot. I'm sorry," he said, grabbing paper napkins by the handful from the table's fake-wood dispenser and doing his best to mop up the mess. "I didn't get you, did I?"

Her smile was wry, as she glanced up from dealing with the muddy drips on her side of the table. "It seems these jeans are destined for the trash."

"I'm really sorry. I'll get you a new pair," he said as Marlene drew close to cluck over and clean up his mess. He thanked her, apologizing again, even as the back of his mind wondered where the heck he could get women's jeans. Ellie would know, but he had no wish to admit this latest failure to his sister.

"You don't need to worry," Lexi said, as soon as Marlene left. "Truly."

"I'm just glad the coffee wasn't hot."

"It's okay. Really."

The genuineness in her answer brought a thickening to his throat. There was something so soothing about this woman, that he could act like a clumsy fool and yet she didn't seem to mind. In fact, if her eyes were to be believed, he might think that she could see the man he wanted to be. The man he knew he couldn't be. But someone he still would try to be, anyway.

Those green eyes studied him now.

"What?"

"You're stressed, aren't you?"

"I'm not."

"Hmm. Not telling the truth, that's what you're not." Her eyes bored into his. "You're worried."

And she was slightly scary in how she could read him. He clearly wasn't wearing his best relaxed cowboy face today. He glanced out the window. Wondered how soon until he could leave. A million things screamed for attention, but he was so weary of everything, it was all he could do to stay upright in the seat.

"Jackson? What's happened?" His attention returned to Lexi. "Is it something to do with the cow the vet came to see?"

"Brutus." Heaviness weighted his shoulders again.

"Oh. Not a cow? The bull, right?"

He nodded, gripping the corner of the table until his wrists hurt. "He's a dud."

She winced. "Oh no. Poor guy."

He wasn't entirely sure if she referred to himself or the bull. Either way felt apt.

"What does that mean for the ranch?"

He couldn't tell her everything and had zero desire to go into all the details of the financial difficulties of the Reilly ranch. But he offered the basics, and must've explained enough, because she nodded, her eyes gentle as she reached her hand across the table and clasped his. "I'm sorry."

For a moment he had the most unmanly inclination to cry.

He pulled away and blinked hard, pinching the outside of his thigh until the sensation passed.

"What can you do?"

"I don't know," he admitted. "Everything is too hard. I need a miracle. The ranch needs a miracle. Mom needs a miracle."

Whoa. He hadn't intended to admit that last thought out loud.

"What kind of miracle does your mum need?"

He swallowed. He didn't want to tell her. Yet he somehow found himself explaining about his mom, about the doctor's assessment earlier this week, which he'd communicated to his brothers who'd seemed as stunned as he was about the diagnosis of possible early-onset dementia.

"We'll need to do some testing, but the signs seem to indicate something of that nature."

Memory loss, confusion, withdrawing from family and friends, changes in behavior were all classic symptoms. The doctor had strongly encouraged more thorough testing, but the thought of pathology tests, neurological exams, brain imaging, and psychiatric assessments, and all the time and money that would involve was enough to do his head in. His visit to the bank to see if there was some way to fund this had instead revealed things were even worse than he'd imagined. And now he had to somehow explain it to Ellie and his brothers.

Her eyes rounded, soft green pools of compassion. "Oh, I'm so sorry."

"The doc was saying she'll likely need a full-time carer soon, or be placed in a facility, but when the bank refuses a loan, well, what can you do?"

She bit her lip, and he was possessed with a sudden savage tug to know her kiss. Which was exactly why he shouldn't be with her. Because, as the bank had proved, he couldn't be trusted with precious things. He seemed to have a way of hurting them or making things worse. And he got the sense that this woman needed something good, someone good, someone in her life who wouldn't leave permanent bruises on her soul like the scar at her throat that her scarf didn't fully hide.

"Can I get you folks anything else?" Marlene asked.

He glanced at Lexi. She shook her head, the slight wrinkle in her brow saying she was still worried about him. He turned to the waitress. "We're fine thanks, Marlene."

She nodded and pushed a docket onto the table. He reached for it, but Lexi was faster. "My treat, remember?"

He shook his head, gesturing for the docket, but she refused to hand it over. "You know that goes against every last fiber in my being."

"Tough."

A chuckle escaped despite himself. Okay, try as he might, he couldn't help but like this girl. She smiled at him then slid from the booth and paid. And sure, a tiny part of him writhed at the fact a woman was paying for his coffee, but another part didn't care. The fact that this woman, *this* woman, seemed to care enough to want to spend time with him made his insides feel like they'd turned to mush. Which wasn't good. Not when the bank had confirmed exactly why he couldn't even dream about getting serious with a girl. Not when the only future he could offer was none at all.

Lexi sashayed back to him, and he couldn't help but notice the way her jeans clung to her hips and legs. "Ready to go?"

He'd been ready to leave town the second Millie at the bank had said no. He nodded, sliding from the booth and following her to the door. He pushed it open, allowing her to walk first, then followed, even as he started focusing on what he'd now need to do. Probably another family consult—Mom's issues were bigger than him—then he'd have to eat some humble pie and admit what a spectacular failure he'd made of everything. Then he'd need to start selling: Brutus, cattle, land. He'd need to call the realtor, see what their options were. Maybe Liam would buy some. He'd always said the Reilly land would be perfect for a solar farm. And it would be—if the owner could afford to pay for the infrastructure. Which clearly Jackson could not.

He paused as he grew aware that Lexi was saying something to him. "Sorry, could you repeat that? I was a million miles away."

"I was wondering if maybe you have another few spare minutes."

He winced. He wanted—needed—to get back, and the longer he stood here with her, the more tongues would wag. Even now he could see old Rhonda Ingalls watching them from across the street. No doubt the gossip lines would be running hot tonight.

"I'm real sorry, but I have to get back to the ranch. I've got a million things to do, and I don't know how to get it done."

Animation drained from her face, and she nodded. He felt like a heel, but exploring things with her was only gonna get them both hurt. Besides, she was going to return to Australia one day. Then where would he be? Left here, picking up the pieces of a broken heart.

But at the sad wash over her features his resolve crumbled. "What was it?"

She shook her head. "It doesn't matter. I'll let you go."

He swallowed, and somehow managed a farewell before pivoting and walking to his truck. He didn't like the finality contained in those words. But then he hadn't liked the words of many people in recent times. Like the vet. Like the doctor. Like the bank manager.

Like the realization that he might have to sell the ranch to save his mom.

CHAPTER EIGHT

She should've told him. She watched the cowboy walk away, her heart berating her for losing courage. How hard was it to say what was on her mind? But ever since his friend-zoning last week, she didn't want to press into his space and demand things he clearly didn't want to give. But the thought that she might hold one of the pieces of his puzzle nagged at her, chasing her to bed, chasing her to sleep, chasing through her dreams.

The next day, she again helped her mother and Sasha, the college cook, who had now returned from vacation. But the feeling that her role here was superfluous to the college needs seemed to follow her around every painted corner. When she was still tossing and turning at two in the morning, she'd finally prayed, committing it to God, asking Him to open the right doors at the right time, if this was indeed the right thing to do.

"Lexi?" her mother called. "Can you come in here, please?"

"Sure."

She found her mother in the great room, eyeing a painting above the grand fireplace. "What do you think? Is it a little too 1980s?"

She stilled. What was she doing here, pretending to be an

interior designer, when a family was obviously in pain, and she could do something about it? "Mum."

"I don't know what to think. Your father and I obviously inherited a lot of things when we took this on, not least of which was the dated decor. But it's never felt right."

"Mum, I need to tell you something."

Her mother held the broom in front of her, like she was trying to block whatever Lexi was about to say. "What is it?"

"I saw Jackson Reilly yesterday."

"I know."

She did? "How?"

"I've had three messages from ladies in the church who thought I might like to know that my daughter was seen on a date with him in the diner."

"It wasn't a date."

"No? You don't call having coffee and eating peach pie with a man a date?"

Gosh, the gossips were good with their details. "I bumped into him down the street. There was nothing planned about it—"

"It doesn't matter. As far as everyone else is concerned, that's what it looked like."

Lexi pushed out a smile at the absurdity of it all. "It's a good thing to see those who live in small towns never engage in idle speculation, isn't it?"

Her mother studied her a moment, then her shoulders dropped. "I'm sorry. I don't know why this bothers me. Jackson Reilly is a nice enough man. He's just got a lot going on."

"He sure does," she murmured, her heart twisting a little as she recalled that lost look in his eyes.

"What is it? Lexi?"

Would it be breaking a confidence to share what she knew? People here seemed to thrive on gossip, and she had no wish to add more. But then Mum had always been someone she could trust. She sucked in a deep breath. "The doctor thinks his mother might have early-onset dementia."

"Oh no."

Lexi nodded. "As he was telling me, I felt an urge to offer to help."

Her mother's lips parted.

"But I didn't," Lexi rushed on to say. "And now I *really* feel like I should say something." *Before it's too late.*

Her stomach clenched. Where had that thought come from?

"But what would you do?" her mother asked.

Her brows rose. "I'm a nurse. I can care for her. And it's not like you need me here."

Her mother's brow wrinkled as she moved to sit down on one of the floral lounge chairs. "You mean you'd move in at the ranch?"

"If they want me. Which they may not, and that's okay. But I have had some training in this area. More than Ellie or Jackson have, I suspect. If it is what the doctor suspects, then I'd be happy to do what I can, which would mean it'd probably be easier if I live there."

"But he's not married."

"And neither is Ellie," she said evenly.

"That's not what I mean."

"If you mean I should be worried about what the town gossips might say, then I'm sorry, but I don't care. The well-being of Mrs. Reilly has to be more important than the small minds and big mouths of others."

"Have you even met her?"

"Mrs. Reilly? No. But then I don't meet most of my patients before I start nursing them."

"What about your work back home? Don't you want to go back?"

"Are you trying to get rid of me?" Lexi tried to joke.

"Not at all! But I don't want you to be limiting your options by staying here, getting caught in a small town you might come to regret."

"I think what I would regret is not offering my assistance when it's obvious I could be of help."

Her mother sighed. "Have you prayed about this?"

She just looked at her mum.

"I take it you have."

"Of course I have. Mum, what would you do in my situation? Aren't we called to love our neighbor as ourselves? I really feel this is what God wants me to do. And who knows? They might say no. Then all the gossips can be none the wiser and you can be happy."

"It's not like that," her mother protested.

Lexi shot another disbelieving look at her mother.

"Okay, perhaps it is."

Lexi gave her a wry smile. "Can I borrow the keys?"

"For what?"

"The car."

"You're not going to drive there, are you?"

"I can't call them. I don't know Ellie's phone number." Focusing on Ellie might be better than focusing on Ellie's brother.

Her mother sighed again. "Are you sure about this?"

"As sure as when I first realized I wanted to nurse."

Her mother studied her a long moment, then finally nodded. "But this won't be forever, will it?"

"I don't know, Mum. But it needs to be now. That much I do know."

"Very well. The car keys are in the kitchen on the rack next to the spices. I won't need it for the next few hours, especially now your father will be back tonight."

Lexi wrapped her mother in a hug. "Thanks, Mum. I'll be back before you know it."

"Hmm. Maybe you should stop in town and see if your new phone is ready yet."

"Good idea."

An hour later, she was driving past the white-fenced Darcy land, her heart hammering. This was so not her usual modus operandi. But still the stubborn thought persisted. She needed to be there. She needed to be there *now*.

She'd only stopped long enough to pack an overnight bag with essentials—just in case the Reillys said yes—and pick up her new phone. And she may have been a little distracted by the bright pink casing—the man had explained they were all out of rose gold—but she wasn't someone addicted to technology, and appearances, apart from her scar, weren't too important to her.

The fence line changed to something more weather-beaten, and the bumps and holes in the road seemed to increase. The Reilly's stone wall entrance drew into view, and she slowed her mum's Toyota, aware she needed to concentrate to make the turn. She might've learned to drive in America, but after years of driving on the left side of the road in Australia, every so often she forgot which side she should be on.

Two minutes later she parked under the pines, hoping no pinecones would drop and leave a dent on Mum's car. That was not the way to gain her mother's support.

"Lord, if you can use me here, then I'm available." Her words bounced around the car's interior. "But please don't let them think I'm being pushy. And if it's all the same to you, I'd really like Jackson not to think I'm doing this for him."

She exited, noting how still and quiet the house appeared, although she could hear the low murmur of voices from an open window. Someone was home. She braced within. Then climbed the steps and knocked on the door.

———

JACKSON CLOSED his eyes as his brothers' voices pummeled through his brain. It was so easy for them. They'd each escaped the ranch to live the life they'd dreamed. And he'd been the patsy, letting them go, fueling their dreams, while he was stuck here working himself to an early grave. He'd found a gray hair last night, ensuring yesterday had ended as it had begun—badly.

"I still don't understand how this could happen," Mitchell said. "What were you and Ellie doing that you never noticed how bad she was getting?"

"We've been busy on the ranch, thank you, Mr. I-only-talk-to-my-family-when-I-don't-have-a-game," Ellie said.

The video call revealed a few smirks from Dermott and Cooper, neither of whom were enamored by their famous brother's insistence that today's meeting take place another time. When Jackson had protested, saying their mother was more important than hockey, Mitchell had instantly replied that of course Mom was more important, and if they had to do it today, could they do it now before his scheduled hockey charity event. Of course, time zones from one side of the country to the other didn't make it easy for Dermott, who was dealing with a new baby, but Mitchell always tended to be a little one-eyed at times.

"I don't remember her being so bad at Christmas," Dermott said.

Jackson knew his eldest brother's relationship with their mom was fraught at best. It had been ever since Dermott had chased his dreams of horticulture instead of taking on the ranch. Dermott's arrival at Christmas with his wife Mindy and stepson Jon had proved an amazingly good reunion. But given the many years that had passed between his visits, it wasn't any surprise the man could barely recognize his own mother, let alone have any clue how much she had deteriorated.

"The doctor has seen that she's changing. He's concerned,

which is why we need to plan what to do next," Jackson said. "Together, as a family."

"I still don't see what the drama is," Cooper said. "So we get Mom to a specialist. Get a nurse in. Whatever. Get it done."

"I'm with him," Mitchell said, yawning. "Look, just pay for it, okay? The ranch can afford it, can't it?"

Jackson stayed silent.

"Jackson?"

He chewed his lip, glanced up at his sister. Knew a crushing weight of disappointment wash over him as he finally said, "Yeah, about that."

"What? What's happened? Why are you looking like that?" Mitchell demanded. "Why is he looking like that, Ellie?"

Ellie shrugged, her frown reflected in her eyes. "I don't know. Jackson?"

He exhaled heavily. "Things aren't going so well here."

"What do you mean?" Cooper demanded. "I thought—"

"Finances have been a little tough lately."

"How tough?" Mitchell asked.

"Tough," he said shortly. So tough, he was expecting the realtor to call in at any time.

"I don't get it."

No. He bet the hockey millionaire didn't have a clue how people in the real world lived.

"So what are you saying?" Cooper asked. "What's happened to the buffer? Isn't the ranch supposed to be in profit by now? I thought that was your plan."

"Plans don't always work out."

"But what about this famous bull of yours? The one who was going to be the baby daddy of half the calves in the neighborhood?"

He swallowed. "He fires blanks."

Cooper blinked. "Are you for real?"

"Yep."

In the silence he heard a faint tapping. Probably the migraine he could feel forming behind his eyes.

"So you spent a ton of money on a stud bull that fires blanks?" Mitchell asked.

Why had he ever boasted about knowing what he was doing? "The vet doesn't know why. She thinks it might be an infection he picked up from somewhere."

"Wow. That's tough," Dermott said. "I'm sorry."

"Yeah."

"Is it treatable?" Ellie asked. "Won't medicine fix him?"

"She doesn't think so."

Jess had said there was a chance that time and yet another round of expensive antibiotics might fix things for poor Brutus —might—but time and money were two things he didn't have.

"Can she be trusted?" Mitchell asked.

"Whoa. This is Jess we're talking about," Cooper protested. "She knows what she's doing."

Both Mitchell and Dermott raised eyebrows, as if wondering why Cooper was so adamant. "Does she? Wasn't she in your year at school?" Mitchell asked.

"So? She's smart. She knows her stuff."

"Her dad has treated our animals for years," Ellie said.

"Yeah, but she's young, and—"

"Are you saying young people can't be trusted?" Ellie snapped, her eyes holding fire.

Mitchell released a world-weary sigh. "I'm just saying why don't you get a second opinion?"

And spend yet more money he didn't have on vets who'd likely say the same thing? Jackson pressed his lips together.

"I don't get it. You told us you knew what you were doing," Mitchell accused. "That we could trust you."

Jackson glanced at the computer keyboard which held a few crumbs from recent meals snatched while he completed work. Why had he put his hand up to take on the ranch responsibility?

"When was the last time you came home, Mitchell?" Ellie asked, her tone demanding.

"You know I have a busy schedule—"

"I know that you have no idea just how hard Jackson works," she snapped.

"He's not the only one." Mitchell leaned back in his chair and folded his arms.

"Yeah? He's the only one who's trying to run a ranch and look after Mom *and* have a life like the rest of you do."

"What do you mean have a life?" Dermott said.

"Oh, you know, meet people," Ellie said, as if Jackson wasn't sitting right beside her.

"Ellie," he muttered.

"People? Like female people?" Dermott asked.

"Who is she?" Cooper asked. "Do I know her?"

"You know Peter Franklin, the director of the Bible college?" Ellie winked at Jackson. "His daughter—"

"You got a girlfriend, bro?" Mitchell leaned towards the screen. "Well, no wonder you're not paying attention to Mom."

"Says the man who couldn't be bothered coming home for Christmas," Ellie

muttered.

"I had a game the next day, or did you forget? Anyway, I sent her a present."

"It's fair enough for Jackson to want to meet someone," Dermott said. "Life can't be all work and no play."

"Yeah, how's that working for you, Dermott?" Cooper said with a smile. "Sick of baby duties yet?"

"It's why I'm the only one of you who knows it's important to balance work with the rest of your life."

And it must be easy for him to say that, living on an island paradise. Jackson stifled the pang of envy, forced himself to wear something that might pass less as a grimace and more as a smile.

"But I still don't get why the ranch isn't doing well. Where'd all the money go?" Cooper asked.

"Bills. Electricity. Feed. Wages. Vet bills. We've had a few tough years, Coop," Jackson said. "But you wouldn't know about that, would you? Not when you're living in an office twenty-four seven." He couldn't help the bitterness in his tone.

"Hey, I get out for at least an hour each day."

"Wow," Dermott said.

Mitchell rolled his eyes.

"He's got no idea, has he?" Ellie muttered.

None of them did.

"Well, you're gonna have to figure something out. We can't let Mom get any worse than she is," Mitchell said. "Why isn't she a part of this conversation?"

"She's asleep," Ellie said.

"At this time of day?" Dermott said. "I always remembered her as being busy, always busy."

His words struck a memory of something Lexi had said just yesterday. Busy, busy, busy. He felt a pain in his heart at how he'd left things. He'd have to make it up to her. Somehow. Yet another thing to add his lengthy list of obligations.

"She wandered off the other day," Ellie said.

"What?" Cooper crossed his arms.

"We couldn't find her for at least an hour. When we did, she was in the machinery shed. I bet she hadn't been there for years."

"She was dressed in her nightgown and had bare feet," Jackson said. "She called me Donald."

As expected, his brothers' jaws dropped. From somewhere he heard the faint sound again, like Miguel was chopping wood or something.

"No way."

Mitchell softly cursed.

"I hate that name," Cooper said, face expressionless.

"She's not good then," Dermott said.

"No."

"And you're telling us there's no money to look after her."

He swallowed. "I'm not saying that."

"Get a nurse," Mitchell said. "I'll pay whatever."

"I'll sort something out." Jackson would rather brand his eyeball than beg for charity from them.

"You better," Mitchell warned. "I don't want to be hearing you've gone and got yourself a girlfriend while letting our mother fade away."

"I don't have a girlfriend. Even if I wanted to—which I don't—I wouldn't have the time." Half true. He didn't have the time. "So would you quit?"

A knock sounded on the door. He stifled a groan. Why couldn't a person be on time instead of insisting on being early? "I need to go. That might be the realtor."

"Are you kidding me?" Mitchell said.

Cooper shook his head. "I can't believe you'd do that without consulting us."

"Consider this me consulting you." Jackson pushed against the headache pounding in his forehead.

"This isn't the way," Dermott said. "We can sort something out."

"You got a realtor?" Ellie looked at him, disappointment shining in her blue eyes.

Aw. Not Ellie. He couldn't stand her looking at him like he'd betrayed her. Even if it felt true. "Just to find out our options."

The knock came again. "I gotta go. Talk again soon."

"But—"

He cut off Cooper's protest with a press of the keyboard.

"Don't open the door," Ellie begged as he rose from his seat. "Whoever it is, say you've changed your mind. The boys are right. This isn't the way."

"I'm sorry, Ellie. We need to know our options."

"I don't want this to be an option," she yelled as he left the room.

Neither did he. But unless God dropped the equivalent of manna from the sky, it seemed his options had just about dried up.

He sucked in a deep breath, shoving his hands through his hair. "God help us."

Then he opened the door.

CHAPTER NINE

Lexi swallowed. "Uh, hi."

Jackson stared at her, and she took that moment to remind her soul that what he'd said two minutes earlier about not wanting a girlfriend wasn't to be taken personally. Even if it felt a little personal. Because right now, this wasn't about him. This was about his mother. She lifted her chin. That's right. She fixed friendliness on her face.

"What are you doing here?"

"Hello to you too, Jackson."

He rubbed his bristly jaw. "I mean, hey, Lexi. I wasn't expecting you."

"I wasn't expecting to be here either."

He half closed his eyes, as if she might be a mirage. "Then what?" He winced.

"You okay?"

"I'm fine," he said.

But it was clear he wasn't. "Do you have a headache?"

"How'd you know?" He pressed the heel of his hand into his forehead, as if he'd like to penetrate his skull.

"I'm a nurse, remember?" She moved forward, forcing him to

take a step back into the dim hall. "You should sit down, close your eyes for a few minutes. Do you get migraines?"

"Sometimes."

"Then maybe you should do what you can to ward it off now."

"I can't. I've got too much to do."

She took another step forward, and he retreated again. "Go. Sit down. Tell me where you keep your ibuprofen."

"Lexi—"

"Sit down." She watched him carefully as he obeyed, moving to a chair positioned next to a low shelf that held rows of muddied boots and outside shoes.

He leaned forward, propping his head in his hands, his elbows resting on his knees.

"Where do you keep your medicine?" she asked as gently as she could.

"Lexi?"

She turned, saw Ellie, whose look of smiled surprise faded as she glanced at Jackson.

"What's wrong with him?"

"Does he get migraines?" Lexi asked softly.

"He sometimes gets headaches, but he never complains."

"I think he has one now. Can you grab some ibuprofen?"

"Uh, sure."

"Wait here," Lexi said, resting her hand on his shoulder briefly, pushing him down as he tried to stand. "No, wait. If you don't want this to get worse, then please do what I say."

He grimaced, but whether that was from the pain or from her words she didn't hang around to find out, instead moving into the kitchen where she collected a glass and filled it with water. A quick glance around the room revealed it needed some attention. Not that she was any great domestic goddess, but she knew clutter and chaos had a way of infecting someone's mind, adding greater pressure. At least it always did to hers.

She returned to the dim hallway at the same time as Ellie. Lexi handed Jackson the glass, and he swallowed the white pills and the water. "Thanks," he muttered.

"You should rest for a few minutes. Maybe in bed."

"Can't." He closed his eyes, tilting his head back and leaning against the wall. "Too busy. Realtor coming. Thought you were him."

Realtor? They weren't going to sell the ranch, were they? Lexi shot Ellie a look. She was biting her lip. Ellie met her eyes and offered a palms-up shrug.

"Okay," Lexi said slowly. "Well, first things first. Jackson, you won't be in any position to talk to a realtor unless your headache is cleared away. So how about you take a few minutes to rest in your room and when the realtor comes we'll let you know. Okay?"

"I'm not a little kid."

"And right now you're not in any fit state to talk about important things or make important decisions. So go. Rest. Ellie will come get you soon."

He peered at her a moment, and seemed about to continue arguing, then he winced. Ellie helped him up and he slowly shuffled away, turning down the hall to what she hoped was his bedroom.

"Wow." Ellie glanced at Lexi, worry in her eyes. "Is he okay? I've never seen him like that before."

Lexi picked up the glass. "Has he had many headaches in the past?"

"If he has, he certainly hasn't told me. And definitely nothing like that before."

"Sounds like he has a lot on his mind."

Ellie exhaled heavily. "You don't know the half of it."

Lexi touched her arm. "Do you need a moment to talk? Sounds like you could do with a listening ear."

Ellie glanced at her, and Lexi caught a shimmer of tears before she blinked them away. "Want a cup of coffee?"

"Love one."

Five minutes later, they were perched on stools at the breakfast bar, drinking coffee that would never be as nice as what Lexi was used to. Even the diner had better coffee than this. If this was what passed as standard, it wasn't surprising so many people added flavors and creamers. They needed to, to disguise the bitterness. But perhaps the shot of caffeine was just what she needed to free her mind of some of the emotional muddle and helping her to hear more clearly what was really being said.

Judging from what Ellie was saying, the chaos lining the kitchen was a sign that all was not well here at the Reilly ranch, and the problems extended far deeper than a mother with possible early-onset dementia.

"So you're saying he needs to sell the ranch to pay the costs?"

"I don't know what Jackson is thinking. Today was the first I've heard of it. We were talking to my brothers, and they were as shocked as me."

"But surely the rest of you have a say in running things. He can't just sell the ranch. This is your family home, isn't it?"

"Yeah." Ellie swallowed the last of her coffee. "But he's the only one who ever wanted to take on the ranch. My other brothers basically left or let him have his way. Even I—" She stopped, glanced down.

"Even you?" Lexi prompted.

Ellie sighed. "It sounds disloyal to say, but sometimes I wonder whether this is all I'll ever do. I mean, I love it here. I really do. But I sometimes wonder what it would be like to travel, to see a little more of the world. Like you have."

"I was able to travel because my dad is from Australia. I grew up there before coming here for a few years. So while I've seen a bit of the world, that was mostly because of family. And you're what, twenty-four, twenty-five? You've got plenty of time to get out and about."

"But that's the thing. I don't know that I ever can. Not when Jackson needs me here. Not when Mom …" She blinked rapidly, and Lexi had a strong sense she was going to cry.

"Hey." She slid off the stool and wrapped Ellie in a hug.

From the way Ellie stiffened, then slowly relaxed until her arms clung on like she'd never let go, it seemed she rarely received hugs. And truth be told, apart from those from her parents, Lexi hadn't received too many hugs in recent times, either. *Lord, please heal the hurts here. Heal Mrs. Reilly. And Jackson.* She swallowed.

Ellie pulled away, wiped under her eyes. "Wow. I wasn't expecting to get teary today."

"What can I help with?"

Ellie threw her hands in the air. "Everything?" She shook her head. "Scrap that. I should be asking what you're doing here today." She smirked, a sparkle of mischief returning to her eyes. "Was it to see Jackson?"

Lexi lifted a hand. "It was, but not like that. We're just friends." And would remain so, especially after overhearing his comment from before. "No, he mentioned something yesterday about your mother not being well, and it made me think about the fact that I'm pretty much sitting around at the Bible College, pretending to help my mother redecorate, when I could be of some use here. If you wanted me to be, of course."

Ellie frowned. "You mean like care for her?"

"I'm a nurse. It's what I do. And while I may not have qualifications that mean I can practice nursing here,"—not yet, anyway—"I still have the training and the experience to help. But that's only if you, Jackson, and your mum are okay with that."

"You'd really come and help?" Hope lit Ellie's eyes.

"I'd hate to be at home twiddling my thumbs when I could be doing something."

"You sound like me and Jackson. We hate sitting around too."

"See? You'd really be doing me a favor, letting me come and help. You'd be saving me from dying of boredom."

Ellie laughed. "I get the feeling you're kinda good at getting your own way."

"If you're calling me manipulative, then I'm prepared to take offense."

"I'm not!" Ellie obviously didn't recognize Lexi was teasing. "I just want to make sure you know what you're getting yourself in for. I don't think we could afford to pay you," she added in a softer voice, regret soft in her eyes.

"That's okay," Lexi whispered back. "I don't think I'm legally allowed to be paid."

"You'd really do it?"

"If you'll have me."

A noise made them turn to see Jackson, one hand on the kitchen door, the look of pain and gray wash on his face from before having eased.

"What are you going to do?" he asked, his gaze shifting between his sister and herself.

Ellie slipped off the stool and smiled at Lexi before pivoting to face her brother. "You're better?"

"Better enough. What's going on here?"

Ellie grinned. "Brace yourself, brother. I think we've found an answer to one of our prayers."

His gaze settled on Lexi, though he spoke to his sister. "What's that?"

"Lexi is going to come here and look after Mom."

———

He blinked, trying to make sense of things, the headache still thudding away inside, although it had eased considerably thanks to a brief nap. But he hadn't been able to rest. His mind kept spinning out of control, thinking, thinking, thinking. But closing his eyes for a few moments had helped ward off the worst of things. Even if he hated lying in bed like a child. He had no intention of ever succumbing to another migraine. Funny how the headaches had increased in recent years.

"Did you hear me?" his sister demanded. Her voice was still a little too loud.

"Are you really feeling better?" Lexi asked, her eyes concerned, her voice far more soothing.

But he didn't want to find her appealing. He couldn't do anything about it. He had to kill any attraction. "I don't need your fussing."

Lexi's eyes widened, as his sister gasped. "Jackson!"

He closed his eyes. "Sorry."

"Lexi came here to offer her help in looking after Mom," his sister snapped. "But I wouldn't blame her if she wanted to walk away. How rude."

He glanced at Lexi again. Her face was sober, her eyes watching him carefully. "I'm sorry. I didn't mean it."

A beat passed. Two. Then she nodded. "It's okay. I truly don't want to be putting myself in the way here, but after our conversation yesterday, I felt convicted to offer my services to help look after your mum. But if you don't want me to that's totally okay." She offered a small smile. "And I genuinely mean that. I have no wish to cause any problems."

He had the feeling she really did mean it. Which made a nice change from all the offense that had been flying around earlier. And all the people he knew who never said what they meant. "We can't afford to pay you."

"And I can't legally be paid on my current visa, so that works out well."

He frowned, and even that movement wrinkled more pain. "Are you saying you'd work for free?" That didn't make sense. Nobody did that.

"Yes."

Huh. Apparently some people did.

"But only if your mum is happy to have me."

He liked how she said the word mom. He liked so many things about this woman. But having her here wasn't good for his peace of mind. Ugh. Who was he kidding? He hadn't had a peace-filled mind for years. Not since he'd come to understand what the weight of responsibility for the ranch meant.

"We should take you in to meet her," Ellie said, as if the decision had already been made.

"But—"

"But what, Jackson?" Ellie said. "You were saying earlier we need a nurse, and a nurse has arrived like an angel from heaven."

An angel dressed in blue jeans and a gray Washington t-shirt.

"Don't you think Lexi might be an answer to prayer?"

"I don't have to stay," Lexi said, putting up her hands. But again he got the feeling that she wasn't miffed or offended. She was simply stating a fact.

"Don't be silly." Ellie dragged Lexi away even as she gave him an "are you serious?" look. "Come meet Mom. Then we can let that decide if she wants you to stay. Honestly." She shot Jackson dagger eyes, and further protest ceased as a knock came at the door.

The realtor. Great. Jackson hurried to the sink and splashed water on his face, willing himself to wake up so he could think more clearly. Why did he feel like everything was slipping out of his fingers?

A moment later he was opening the door, pasting on a smile. "Hey, Bob. Thanks for coming out."

Bob Ingalls was a grizzled old coot, but he'd known the Reilly family forever. And he attended church, which should mean Jackson could trust him. Even if he knew he could trust Rhonda, Bob's wife, to flap her gums.

They shook hands. "Never thought I'd see the day." Bob looked around.

"Come in."

He wished he'd had a chance to spruce the place up a bit. Seeing it through someone else's eyes—Bob's and, now he thought about it, Lexi's—he realized just how tired and rundown the house looked. But it met their needs and had served their family well. Besides, today wasn't about trying to make good impressions but seeing if there was any way to salvage something of the ranch while getting some money for land they didn't use.

"Come on in." Jackson cleared papers off the office's spare chair before pulling out the file that held the property deeds.

"I gotta ask upfront: why am I talking to you and not your mom?" Bob asked. "Isn't she the rightful owner?"

The rightful owner was actually the man who had disappeared over two decades ago. But there was nothing right about that man having any say in the ranch's future. Not when he'd made it clear he didn't want to be a part of theirs.

"Mom isn't well. And as you know I've been looking after things for the past ten years or so."

"Uh huh." Bob eyed him with a look that said he saw more than Jackson wanted. "What about your pa?"

"What about him?"

"Does your dad know about this?"

"Why would he?"

Bob's eyebrows plummeted. "Have you spoken to the man at all?"

"Not a word since he ran out of here. Nobody's seen hide nor hair of him in years. I was given power of attorney after he was declared legally dead, remember?"

"I do."

Jackson drew in a deep breath, bracing for further argument.

"Well, it can't hurt to just talk, now, can it?" Bob leaned back in his chair.

"No, sir. Like I said on the phone, it'd be helpful to know what our options are."

Bob nodded. "Have you got a site survey, like I asked?"

Jackson handed it over. "Right here."

Jackson studied the man, his heart thudding louder than the wicked pulse in his brain, as Bob frowned and nodded and ahemed. "So the property borders the Darcy estate all this way." He showed Jackson the map and drew a line down the western side.

"Yep."

"Part of that fancy experimental ranch, huh?" He shook his head. "I sure don't understand nonsense like that."

So it seemed Bob was one of those die hards who weren't fans of environmental causes.

"Thought about selling off some to him?"

"Maybe." For some reason he didn't want to tell Bob everything he thought.

"You do have a pretty piece of land here. I reckon it'd sell better as one lot, but I can see that there would be potential to maybe subdivide. But I gotta be honest. I don't think you're gonna get a lot of people wanting a smallholding out here. Especially not with that new estate closer to town in Trinity Lakes."

"Surely there would be some people who'd like more rural views."

"Mebbe. But I can't guarantee anything." Bob's frown had moved to his eyes. "You don't have all the town services out here, do you? Electricity, town water, sewerage."

"We have electricity." This wasn't exactly *Survivor*.

"But not the other two. Hmm. That's gonna cut down potential interest." Bob glanced up and studied Jackson with that same look of foreboding. "Most folks like the idea of running a ranch. Doing real ranch things ain't always their cup of tea."

"I understand that."

"Do you? Because if you do, then you might see that where you're proposing to divide the land might not work as well as if you squared off a piece next to the Darcy land." His eyebrows rose. "Have you thought about selling this place?"

"The house?"

"I'll be honest. I don't think this older style is necessarily what buyers are looking for. But if you gave it a quick spruce up, maybe painted, recarpeted, new kitchen fit outs, you might be able to get a prettier penny."

Spend money they didn't have on paint, a new kitchen, and carpets? "That's something to keep in mind." Jackson hoped his tone sounded more relaxed than he felt.

"Want to show me around the place?" Bob smiled. "I didn't see much when you had your New Year's Eve shindig. All I remember is it being plenty dark and cold."

"Come this way, then."

But when he reached the hall, it was to see Ellie. She eyed Bob with an unfriendly expression, something which became a true glare as she turned to Jackson.

"Well, now, Miss Ellie. It's been a while," Bob said.

"Sure has." Her voice was tight. "Just so you know, not all of us are in agreement that this is what should happen."

"What will happen?" Bob asked, sounding puzzled. "Let me tell you, I'm only here doing a favor for a friend. I sure don't want to be making anybody feel bad. By the same token, if it means I can help you out, then that's what good neighbors are for, right?"

His comment dug deep, shifting Jackson's thoughts to the other person who had arrived today, willing to be a good neighbor. But she had made it clear she'd be taking no cut. "Excuse me for a moment, Bob. If you want to head into the yard, I'll be there in a moment."

"Sure thing."

As he opened the glass door Jackson turned to his sister. "Where's Lexi?"

"In with Mom." She smiled. "Mom seems to like her, so I left them to get acquainted."

"Are you sure that's a good idea?"

"Jackson, she saved Jordan's life. I think it's safe for Mom to be with her." Her eyes frowned. "You on the other hand …"

"What do you mean?"

"I don't think you're making wise decisions today. And I have to admit, I don't like Bob being here, looking around at everything like he's pricing it. I bet he's going to go home and tell Rhonda about all our problems."

"He wouldn't do that."

"You think? Half the gossip of Trinity Lakes is spread by that woman. I really don't like him being here."

"It's too late now."

She shook her head. "I really think this is a dumb idea."

His chest grew tight. He hated disappointing his sister. Hated having her think less of him. "He's waiting for us."

"Hmm. Maybe Fido will eat him."

"Ellie."

"What? Don't hate me for not wanting to sell."

"Nobody is saying anything about selling things today."

"But you may in the future?"

Exasperation heated his chest. "We need a way to survive, Ellie. The ranch needs to run in the black, not the red."

"I just don't think this is the right way. Are you trusting God? Hasn't He provided with an answer for Mom?"

"If this even works out," he said.

"Who is to say it won't? I thought you liked Lexi. Why are you so resistant to her working here?"

"It's not safe."

"For who? For her?"

"For me."

She studied him. "I don't get it."

"If she's here, and if she stays here, then what do you think all the gossips will say? They'll think she's my girlfriend, that she's living in sin or something. I don't want to do that to her."

"You wouldn't be," she said. "That's on them, not on you."

But it felt like it would be his fault, something else he'd bear the blame for. And worse than that, if he didn't take care, he might find himself doing something he wanted to do but knew he shouldn't.

Like kissing Lexi.

CHAPTER TEN

"Mrs. Reilly? Would you like me to make you a cup of coffee?"

Stringy gray hair blew around the older woman's face as she turned to Lexi. "Thank you."

Lexi squatted beside the bed, covering the woman's hand with her own. "Do you like it with milk and sugar?"

"Black is fine, no cream or sugar."

"I'll be right back."

She returned to the kitchen, glad for the chance to exhale and breathe in some fresher air. Mrs. Reilly's room could do with a good airing and a deep clean, like much of the rest of the house. But she knew that was something that could be dealt with another time. Right now was all about trying to establish some kind of a bond with this woman who had birthed and raised Jackson and Ellie. So far things seemed to be going well, but having nursed other patients with similar kinds of symptoms, she knew it didn't take long for things to become strained.

She switched on the coffee-maker, then glanced out the window. Jackson and Ellie stood with an older man, the realtor, or so Ellie had assumed before she'd rushed out, complaining about her brother's illogical state. She didn't seem any happier now, standing there with a scowl and crossed arms.

But Jackson had Lexi's sympathy. She'd seen the way he'd looked yesterday, the wash of sadness on his features something she couldn't forget, now seemingly seared onto her heart.

"Lucy?" Mrs. Reilly's faint call came.

Huh? Oh. "Coming!"

She filled the mug and added a trace of sugar. Mrs. Reilly was mere skin and bones, like she hadn't eaten properly for weeks. She needed fattening up, and perhaps the sugar would help sweeten her mood.

"Here you go." She placed the mug on the wooden bedside table, the clutter atop now a little more straightened. She would normally look for a coaster to protect the wood, but the many round dark stains suggested coasters weren't a priority.

"Thanks." Faded blue eyes followed Lexi as she moved around the room to take a seat on the chair. "Who are you again?"

"Lexi."

"Jackson's girlfriend?"

Lexi choked. "No, ma'am. I'm Ellie's friend. And Jackson's too, but it's nothing like that."

Mrs. Reilly's chin dipped, but the eyes remained fixed on Lexi. She stared back. She could see a vague resemblance to Jackson in the nose and curly hair, but the eyes were different, more like Ellie's.

"Would you like me to open the windows?" Lexi took the shrug as acquiescence, and moved to open the windows, taking care to make sure the midday light didn't fall directly on the bed. Truth be told Mrs. Reilly was probably healthy enough to not need to be in bed, but it was obviously where she felt more comfortable. Lexi wasn't about to upset her, not on her first day here. She spent a moment surreptitiously tidying, then moved to the closet. "Would you like me to put these clothes away?"

No answer, which Lexi took as affirmation. She picked up a shirt which would further crease if not hung up, and moved to the closet.

"Why are you here?"

Lexi paused, coat-hanger in hand, one hand on the closet door. "I'm here to help."

"Help? How?"

"Your daughter, Ellie, asked me to."

"Ellie." A vertical line creased Mrs. Reilly's forehead. "She likes history."

"That's right."

"Jackson."

Lexi stilled. Was he here? She hung up the shirt, then peeked at the door. No Jackson to be seen. Maybe it was safe to let Mrs. Reilly's observations continue as she wished. "What about him?"

"He likes horses."

"Yes."

"He's a good boy."

Lexi nodded, ducking her head as the backs of her eyes burned. Those four words somehow seemed so special, such an endorsement from mother about her son that Lexi felt like she was almost treading on sacred ground. If only Jackson could hear his mother's esteem. Would he be so quick to want to sell the ranch?

"He doesn't visit often," Mrs. Reilly continued.

"I think it is because he's busy working around the ranch."

"Always busy," Mrs. Reilly said, hand plucking at the covers. "Likes his lists."

"Does he?" Jackson hadn't seemed the type to like lists. But now she thought about it, there seemed some method to his approach, a focus that sometimes seemed to be seeking what was next, rather than focusing on the immediate and now.

"Like his father."

Lexi stilled. From what had been said before, it seemed

discussion about Mr. Reilly was problematic. But before she could enquire further there came a loud barking—Fido?—and voices as brother and sister and realtor returned. "Excuse me for a moment."

Mrs. Reilly didn't make any acknowledgement that she had heard Lexi speak, so she took that as permission to leave. She moved into the hallway, gently closing the door behind her. The glass sliding door clicked closed in the next room.

"Well, that's been most informative," an unfamiliar older man's voice said. "I'll give it some thought and send something through. I'm sure we can come to some arrangement."

Her chest thudded. Surely Jackson hadn't decided to sell? There had to be another way.

"I'd appreciate that," Jackson said.

"Mr. Ingalls, you know we haven't agreed yet." Ellie's tone held a polite kind of fierceness, as if she was holding onto good manners by the skin of her teeth.

"I'm aware of that, little lady—"

Ugh. Lexi grimaced. Such condescension.

"—and like I said to your big brother here, we'll continue this conversation."

She heard a step creak, then before she could move from the hall, she was facing an older man. "Well, now, and who do we have here?"

"Bob, this is—"

"Lexi Franklin." She drew closer. "And you are?"

"Bob Ingalls, at your service."

She nodded, although she doubted he would ever be of service to her.

"And what are you doing here?" Bob asked, one brow raised quizzically.

She glanced behind him to where Ellie's rolled eyes and Jackson's small frown suggested they didn't care for the man's intrusive manner any more than she did. "I'm a friend."

"A friend with an accent." He glanced at Jackson and Ellie. "Am I to guess whose friend, and what kind of friend she may be?"

Ugh. Any liking she might try to have for the man faded. "Apparently."

He stared at her, as Ellie's attempt to muffle a chuckle failed. Jackson's lips twitched as he glanced at her then cleared his throat. "Well, Bob, I don't want to keep you."

"Hmm." Bob eyed Lexi before giving her a small nod of dismissal as he turned and followed Jackson out the door.

"Wow." Ellie pulled her ponytail tight. "That man."

"He seems a little nosy."

"You should meet his wife. Rhonda Ingalls. On second thought, maybe don't. She's one of the notorious gossips of Trinity Lakes." Ellie rolled her eyes. "I mean, I know we're supposed to love all people, but man, she makes it hard to even like her."

"People with small lives like to gossip about others." Or so Dad used to say.

"Then her life must be tiny."

They swapped smiles. "How did things go?"

Ellie's sigh could've stripped wallpaper. "I don't think everything is as bad as Jackson thinks, but what would I know? I'm just the annoying little sister pointing this out."

"Whose life is affected by these decisions."

"Right?" Another eye roll.

"Have you looked at the books?"

"Math isn't really my thing."

"Is there an accountant?"

"There is, actually," Jackson's voice came from behind her. "Mr. Thomas was the one who first pointed out that our expenditure exceeds our income."

Heat rushed up her cheeks as she saw the frown had extended into his posture. "I didn't mean—"

"Is there a reason you're here and not with my mom?"

"She's fine."

"Is she? How would you know?"

"Jackson," Ellie protested. "Lexi came out just a moment ago."

He exhaled and glanced away. From the pulse throbbing in his cheek, she guessed he was trying to keep his temper under control.

"I'm sorry if you think I spoke out of turn," she said, looking at Ellie when it became clear he wasn't going to look at her.

"Honestly, Jackson, I can't believe you're treating Lexi this way. She's doing us a favor."

He crossed his arms. "How has my mother been?"

"She's been fine. Look, come say hello." Lexi strode to the end of the hall and opened the door, then gasped. "Mrs. Reilly? Oh my goodness!"

The poor woman had fallen, and now lay half sprawled out of the bed.

———

"MOM!" Jackson pushed past Lexi as he rushed to his mother's aid, wrapping an arm around her shoulders as he helped her back into bed. "Are you okay? Did you hurt yourself?"

"I spilled my coffee." His mother's voice was whispery thin.

A brown patch was creeping across the bedsheets, and he shot Lexi a look.

"I'm so sorry. She was fine five minutes ago." She bent to collect the mug.

He helped his mother shift up against the pillows, and with a hissed "Ellie!" got his sister to help change the sheets. It felt humbling to be doing so, the woman who had given life to him looking so frail and thin in the bed. Clearly Lexi wasn't doing what she should. This wouldn't work. Something else would need to happen.

Regrets pushed against his chest, his failures pounding inside like a toxic cocktail. His time with Bob—with Ellie in full raging guardian bulldog mode—left him feeling even more antsy. And his hope of having one thing in his life sorted—his mom—now made him only too aware how fast her life could slip between his fingers. And judging from the weight of disappointment, his hopes for something with Lexi had been higher than he'd realized.

"I'm really sorry, Mrs. Reilly," Lexi said again. "I should get you a bell or something."

"A bell?" He shot her a look of disbelief. "You should've been here."

"Stop being unreasonable," Ellie said. "Mom had an accident. Accidents happen. Deal with it."

"I would've thought a professional nurse would know how to prevent an accident," he said, hating the words coming out of his mouth, but unable to stop them. "Is that what happened before?" He motioned to his neck. "Was that an accident too?"

Lexi straightened, her cheeks paling as her lips parted. She swallowed, the ripple in her throat drawing attention to the edge of a scar her slipped scarf could no longer hide.

"Jackson!" Ellie's anguished look said he'd gone too far. "You need to apologize."

But before he could, Lexi held up a hand, and his remorse was trapped in his throat.

"Mrs. Reilly, it was very nice to meet you today."

"You too, dear."

Lexi smiled, but even he could tell it was an effort.

Remorse twisted within. "Lexi, I'm—"

"I'm sorry things haven't worked out," Lexi said to his mother, even as he got the sense the words were meant for him. "I do hope you feel better soon. I'll be praying for you."

"Lexi, please don't go," Ellie begged.

Lexi refused to meet his eyes as she patted Mom's hand and picked up the cup and what looked like her purse. "I'm going to let your mother have some rest." She moved past Ellie and out the door.

Ellie shot him a look then hurried after her. Leaving him with his mom, who looked at him. "What is it, Mom? Are you okay?"

"I'm okay."

"Then why are you looking at me like that?"

"I like her."

So did he. And he had a feeling he'd just screwed everything up big time. "I'll be back in a moment, okay?"

"Go get her, Tiger."

He blinked at her. How long had it been since he'd heard her use that expression? Except Mom had never used it about a girl.

"Go on."

He hurried from the room, following the voices outside to where Lexi was opening her car door. "Lexi, wait."

"No. You should go." Ellie shot him a death laser glare. "I don't want you anywhere near my awful brother right now."

"I didn't mean it," he said, moving closer to hold onto the car door. "Please, forgive me."

She glanced away, and he noted the curve of her cheek and jaw, the creamy color of her skin. Five freckles dotted the milkiness of her collarbone before it disappeared under her t-shirt.

"Lexi." He touched her hand, saw her startle as if his touch electrified as it did him. Still her gaze remained averted. "Please. Let me explain."

Finally she turned to face him, and he was confronted by a shimmer in those green eyes. His heart twisted, as regret upon regret boiled within. He'd made her cry? "I'm sorry. So sorry." He glanced at his sister, motioned to shoo her away. But she only arched a brow and crossed her arms, remaining exactly where she was.

Fine, then. "Lexi, I'm really sorry for what I said in there. I didn't mean it. I guess I'm just stressed about all of this, and Bob—"

His sister snorted.

"Having Bob here, knowing he's seen you, and that he's likely to tell others you were here—"

"Like his wife," Ellie said. Lexi's eyes widened.

"I'm trying to do my best, but I keep falling short, and—" His voice cracked, and he heaved in a breath and rubbed a hand over his face. "I can't get anything right today."

He released the car door and turned away, scuffing his boot on the dusty driveway as he sucked in air to try to regain composure. He was an idiot, chasing away the one good thing that had happened today.

The breeze's coolness whispered against his skin as he put his hands on his hips and surveyed the ranch, seeing it as Bob had. Bob had not been shy about offering his opinion. "It needs a lot of work, son. I'm sorry, but I don't think you can expect top dollar, not if we're going to be realistic. If you want to sell, you need to be aware that while the market has been hot and prices have been generous, it's not a guarantee. And judging from the land and the condition of the house and barn and outbuildings, I'd be lying if I said I believed I could get a buyer for anywhere near what you'd be asking."

So selling was a bust. At least for the price Jackson had believed the property was worth. The price Bob had mentioned had been so low Jackson had nearly laughed at him. Nearly. Except that part of him which had kinda wanted to cry.

"Jackson."

He pivoted at the soft voice. Hope rose as Lexi studied him seriously. "I am very sorry. You must know that."

"I do." He held out a hand. "Can we start over?"

Her gaze fell to his hand, then travelled back up again, and she finally lifted her fingers to meet his.

His fingers wrapped around hers, even as electricity zapped between them. "Friends?"

She licked her bottom lip, and he was taken with another stupid urge to know her better, to kiss her even. As if she'd see him like that. The best he could hope for was—

"Friends."

She stared up at him, and he experienced fresh regret at having made the dumb comment about her throat. This woman was incredibly gracious to him, far more than he deserved. He'd have to make things up to her. *Lord, help her to forgive me. Help me make things up to her.*

"Did you ... do you still want to leave?" He wished Ellie wasn't still on sentry duty.

"Are you asking her to stay?" his annoying sister asked, hands on hips.

"Yes." He studied Lexi. "Please stay. Mom likes you. She told me so. And I'd hate you to think I don't want you around. Because I do." He really did. Maybe a little too much.

Lexi's lips tugged north half an inch, and her chin lifted a fraction. "You can trust me," she finally said. "I know, better than anyone, that I'm not perfect, but I'd never compromise my patient's safety. You've got to believe me."

"I do." Again that word sounded like a promise of something more. He gently squeezed her hand, and she glanced at their clasp as if finally noticing their hands were still joined. "I want you to stay. Please."

She peeked across at Ellie, who gave an encouraging nod, as if she too was feeling this was one of those pivotal moments, when futures balanced precariously and could flip either way. Heads, he'd win. Tails, he'd lose. And not just in terms of their friendship or his mother's health and care. There was something about this woman that seeded hope within, that helped him feel like life, the ranch, his future actually had possibilities. How he hoped she might say yes. *Please, God.*

She bit her lip, and he knew he'd have to guard himself. The attraction he felt for her would never work, not if they were staying in the same house and sharing meals and sharing space and …

"Lexi?"

Ellie's voice snapped his thoughts back to the present, and he nodded. "Please? For my mom's sake?"

CHAPTER ELEVEN

Lexi checked on Mrs. Reilly, the dim light from the hall falling over her sleeping features. The past three days had seen the lows of that first day lift to something more stable. Lexi would drive to the ranch each morning, then back to the college again to sleep, then repeat the trip again the next day. Ellie had noted Lexi's tiredness and insisted she could stay, that Mitchell's room was spare, and it would make a lot more sense for her to stay each night than drive home in the dark.

So she'd agreed and was staying overnight for the first time, allaying her mother's fears by promising she wasn't there for any reason than simply to care for Mrs. Reilly. At least things there were getting easier. Mrs. Reilly let Lexi take her to the bathroom and help her shower now. And if extra time here meant a little tidying up along the way, she hoped nobody would be so petty-minded as to hold that against her. Even if that person had made it very clear she was of no interest to him save in how she treated his mother.

Lexi breathed a prayer, then gently closed the door, and returned to the kitchen. Ellie was watching an archeology lecture on a laptop in the attached dining room, and Jackson was nowhere to be seen. If Lexi had any thought he might have interest, as some of his long looks and hand-holding seemed to have suggested, then the fact he'd barely spoken to her in the past few days had made it very clear. He wasn't interested. She'd obviously been imagining things to have thought otherwise. Which was fine. She was here for his mother, not for him.

"… going well." Jackson's voice trickled to her, probably from the room she'd discovered was his office. A bomb site, more like. She didn't understand how anyone who apparently liked checklists could live in such a pigsty. The one time she'd accidentally visited—looking for something Ellie said she needed—had almost given her hives, the mess and chaos stressing every molecule inside. What she'd give for a good few days to clean the room.

"Nope. That's worked out too. She's much calmer now."

She glanced at Ellie, but she had her headphones on, watching intently. Really, someone should pay for the girl to go to university.

"Yeah, we got a nurse. She's really good."

Well, that was something. After practically begging her to stay, she'd been kind of surprised when he'd said nothing more. The fact he found her efforts worth commending drew a warm glow in her heart.

"No," Jackson said, to whomever it was he was talking to. Probably one or more of his brothers, if Ellie's comment earlier at dinner was true. "She must be mid-twenties."

Who? Oh. She inched closer to the open door.

"If you must know, her name is Lexi, and no, she's not my type."

A slash across her chest revealed something she hadn't wanted to explore.

"I mean it. She's—"

"Lexi?"

She rushed back to the kitchen, wiping her hair back in a

pose she hoped conveyed nonchalance, as Ellie appeared, yawning. "Hey, is your lecture done?"

"Yeah." She nodded to the office. "Is Jackson in there?"

"Yep."

"I suppose I should go talk to my brothers, although I'd rather watch a chick flick with you." She sighed. "You've got no idea how glad I am to have another woman around. I mean, there's Mom, of course, but she's not exactly around, if you know what I mean."

She knew.

"And honestly, growing up with four brothers, I'm surprised I got to do any girlish things at all. You're so lucky to only have one brother."

Part of tonight's enticement had been a promised movie from their huge DVD collection. Of course, most of them were action movies, but there had been a few westerns and some older romances too. When Lexi had commented on the latter, Ellie had said her mom used to enjoy watching them when she'd got a chance. Which was rare, except for winter nights, given the time-drain that was the ranch.

"Anyway, the bathroom is free if you want it. If this phone call is anything like the last one, it's gonna take forever."

"Okay, thanks."

She was tempted to follow Ellie in and introduce herself to whoever was on the other end of the call but figured that probably wasn't the best way to make a good impression. Instead, she moved back to the room she was sleeping in—Mitchell's room, complete with clear plastic boxes of what looked like old hockey trophies stacked up against one wall. She gathered her clothes and moved to the shower. After the heat of the day, she could really do with washing her hair.

Half an hour later, the dirt of the day sufficiently cleaned away, she spat out her toothpaste, took a drink, and studied her reflection in the patch of fogged glass she'd wiped clear. A pale face and freckles and big eyes stared back. She angled her neck. The curved neckline of the "Cat's Pajamas" PJ top was almost a perfect match for the red curve across her throat. Memories flashed. She suppressed them. She had no desire to revisit that moment unless absolutely necessary. And given it would never be absolutely necessary to share what had happened, she'd be best to forget it, even if she'd never stop wearing turtle-necked tops.

"Lord, I really don't want to be so self-conscious about it all the time," she whispered.

Maybe she could let her scar be seen. But wouldn't that open her up for more unwanted comments like Jackson's comments the other day? She still couldn't believe he'd been so carelessly dismissive. An accident? If only he knew. And if only he knew how much his words had stung, how she had tossed and turned as his words writhed through her sleep.

But thoughts about Jackson never led anywhere good. She'd be better off grabbing her e-reader and finding a fictional man to dream over.

She collected her belongings, opened the door, and collided with a solid chest. "Oh!"

Hands grabbed her upper arms, and she looked up to see the man she'd vowed not to think about. "Are you okay?"

Call her crazy, but it seemed like time slowed, like the air between them was charged, like every particle or neutron or whatever it was had suspended in this moment. Jackson still had his hands on her arms, his eyes remained on hers, his lips parted. And then his gaze slid to her mouth, where it stayed for a long time before sliding further down, to her chin, then coming to rest at her throat.

She felt exposed, naked, even though she was fully clothed. Why hadn't she worn a bathrobe? Or covered up a little more?

"Lexi." Jackson's voice was raspy, deep, and holding a hint of husky drawl before his eyes lifted to meet hers. "I ... I ..."

He leaned closer, his gaze dropping to her mouth.

Her pulse ratcheted up. Was he going to kiss her? She wet her bottom lip, saw his gaze snag there, and felt her body sway to his.

He lifted a hand, and with a touch of his hand as gentle as the dawning sun over hills, drew two fingers down her skin, down to the corner of her mouth, where his finger paused.

"You have some toothpaste."

What? His words broke the connection, and she backed away, but he drew closer, his finger still next to her mouth, their strange dance ending as she backed into the wall.

His pupils dilated in the hallway's dimness as he caressed the spot with his fingertip. His face bent lower. Breath suspended as his hand slid down her jaw to linger at her throat. His gaze met hers, as if wondering if he could touch her there. She tilted her chin slightly as permission.

Heat traversed her throat as he gently traced her scar, his expression soft, his touch tender. Nobody, save herself, her mum, and several doctors, had touched her there since the incident.

"I'm so sorry this happened to you."

Whether it was from the rasp of sincerity in his voice, or the intensity of his gaze, emotion clogged until she wanted to cry. She drew in a shaky breath, working to stifle the tears. Why was he being so kind? Just what had wrought this change?

His gaze lifted and his hand slid back up her cheek, then, as if aware of just what he'd been doing, he blinked and shifted away. "Sorry. I don't know why I did that."

"I thought I wasn't your type," she murmured, eyes fixed on him.

"What?" His gaze dropped to her mouth, then back up again.

"You said I wasn't your type. On your call tonight."

The air between them cooled as he inched further away. "You heard that?"

She nodded, and something that looked awfully like regret flashed across his features. "I'm not good at this stuff." He shoved a hand through his hair.

"What stuff?"

"Girls. You. Saying the right thing. Having you here. I mean, I'm glad you're here, really glad—"

Judging from the past few moments of tenderness, she'd kinda got that idea.

"—but I just don't know."

He didn't know? Didn't know what? Hadn't that been attraction pulsing between them not fifteen seconds earlier?

He backed away, crossing his arms, as if protecting himself from her. She couldn't help but notice his biceps bulged. "I know I keep messing up. I probably shouldn't have touched you like that. I don't know what came over me."

She drew her toiletries bag and her day's clothes to cover her chest, wishing she had a way to cover her throat that wouldn't look obvious.

"I guess it's the fact I finally saw your scar properly and realized that whatever happened must have been so traumatic. And I made that stupid comment about it the other day. Anyway, I'm sorry. I'm really sorry."

Her pulse thundered in her ears. "It's okay."

"Is it?"

His gaze searched hers, a kind of desperation in the dark depths until she finally nodded.

His features relaxed. "I know I'm probably the last person you ever want to talk to about things, but if ever you'd like to talk, well, I can be a listening ear."

Somehow she found herself wanting to tell him. The words burned in her chest, but a noise in the hall drew attention to Ellie, who was staring at them like she was watching a magic show.

"Ellie!" Lexi tried to move back, but she'd pretty much be

pushing a hole through the wall. And from what she'd seen of this place, that might not be too difficult. Ellie had said the realtor had suggested the place needed new paint and carpet. Lexi was pretty sure it needed way more attention than that.

"What are you two doing?"

"Nothing," Jackson said from his side of the hall.

"Talking," Lexi said.

"Uh huh." Ellie glanced between them, her upraised brows suggesting she wasn't buying. "Sure didn't look like that."

Lexi swallowed, perversely pleased to see by his dipped Adam's apple that Jackson was affected too. "I don't know what you think you saw, but I'm going to bed."

"Hmm. And Jackson's going to have a cold shower. Am I right?"

"You're annoying, that's what you are," he said.

Lexi bit back a smile, offered the siblings a goodnight, and finally moved past Jackson, taking care to not look at him at all. But when she went to close her door, she couldn't help but notice he was still there in the hallway, his gaze on her door. Her mouth didn't obey her brain, and she flashed him a smile.

He grinned back.

Her heart soared, the lightest it had been all week.

For all his denials and protests, she got the feeling that maybe, just maybe, Jackson Reilly might like her a little bit after all.

———

JACKSON CLASPED his hands behind his head as he stared up into darkness. He shouldn't have touched her. He had to get away. But even lying here in the bunkhouse, putting a quarter mile's worth of distance between them, wasn't far enough. He couldn't stop thinking about her, her lips, her curves, her scar. The unexpected joy of seeing her had filled him with a greedy rush of pleasure, something that had been happening more and more lately, his senses straining for her, hungry for her presence, her voice, her smile, her scent. And then to see her last night in his house, makeup free, hair damp, looking oddly vulnerable with nothing hiding that awful scar, he'd had the weirdest sense of wanting to kiss it better.

And now, after Ellie had busted them in that dangerous encounter in the hallway, he knew he couldn't stay in the house too. Lexi's reputation would never survive. So he'd put distance between them. Not that he'd ever be inclined to do anything ungentlemanly, but this way nobody could accuse him of such things.

So after Lexi had smiled at him from the door of Mitchell's old room, and he'd done his best to explain to his sister that he hadn't been trying to kiss Lexi—which was probably a lie, but he couldn't explain his behavior himself—he'd grabbed a sleeping bag and his pillow and headed outside to the bunkhouse where he could be safe.

Except he wasn't. For he couldn't stop thinking about her. Wishing ...

Breath escaped, loud in his ears.

He rolled to his side, thoughts churning through his brain. His conversation with his brothers. They'd been relieved when he'd told them Bob hadn't proved the goldmine Jackson had imagined he might be. He got the impression that Cooper's old cynicism was hard at work. Cooper wouldn't trust any realtor to give them a price worth the years of memories, let alone Bob. Maybe he should contact Liam Darcy again. But he was in Africa, out of reach. Still, it wouldn't hurt to see if the man might be interested in the piece of land down near the Darcy solar farm. Even if his brothers were adamant he should never carve up the land Reillys had ranched for generations.

"God, what else can I do?" His muttered prayer filled the empty space.

His brothers certainly had a lot of opinions. After telling him exactly what they thought about his efforts with the land, they'd started on Mom. At least that had been a better result. For his concerns about Mom had eased—she seemed happier and more settled, even if her nurse made him feel the opposite. Well, not unhappy exactly—how could he be unhappy when Mom was being cared for, and the house was looking cleaner?—but maybe just a little anxious. When his brothers had asked about Mom's nurse, he'd lied again, saying Lexi meant nothing to him. But tell them the truth and suffer through the inevitable teasing? No thanks. A man had enough to live down and didn't need to go courting more. He groaned.

And she'd heard it. Judging from that last comment, she'd been unimpressed by his lie. Which obviously was a lie based on the way he'd nearly kissed her, the way he now dreamed of her, imagining what her lips would taste like ...

He rolled to the other side, pulling out the sleeping bag so it fit more comfortably. How many years had it been since he'd slept in such a thing? He was grateful that at least the space wasn't as uncomfortable as he might've first supposed. Not that he'd ever thought the bunkhouses uncomfortable—their workers had always expressed their appreciation at the standard, which was apparently higher than comparable ranches—but it wasn't exactly his bedroom back in the main ranch building. The rooms were fairly spacious and had ensuite bathrooms, so people didn't have to brave the cold and snow in mid-winter treks. His grandfather had known what he was doing when he'd upgraded things back in the early nineties. Still, it wouldn't take much to upgrade the room to the standard of a basic motel. Assuming people wanted to experience a taste of ranch life. Something someone once said hovered around the recesses of his mind, and he closed his eyes trying to chase it down, but his brain was as settled as a black-tailed jackrabbit, too busy with thoughts of the ranch, finances, Brutus, Mom. Lexi.

The plaintive "aaarooom" of a distant cow startled him to greater wakefulness. This was dumb. Maybe he'd be better off doing something. Even if it was a big day tomorrow—today—completing chores he'd prefer not to leave for Sunday.

He shucked off the sleeping bag, threw on a light sweater and long sweats, shoved his feet into boots—fashion statement, not—and moved out to the barn, his phone's torch lighting the way. Not that he really needed it as he could walk this route in his sleep, but nobody needed to be stepping into a pile of Fido's mess, especially at this hour of the morning.

At the barn he drew open the door, moving quietly inside to where Brutus was penned. "Hey, boy."

The animal snuffled at his hand, and Jackson rubbed his head, the coarse hair springy to his touch. "I'm sorry you're still stuck in here. I bet you'd rather be with your lady friends, huh?"

Talk like that was likely to take his mind places it shouldn't, so he did what he'd started doing a week or so ago. "Dear Lord, please heal Brutus, make him whole again. Amen."

They needed a miracle, and God was the ultimate miracle-giver.

"Ahem."

Jackson yelped and spun around, squinting against the glare of a torch. "Denny?"

"I saw a light, boss. Didn't think it'd be you."

"Who did you think it'd be if not me?"

Denny shrugged as he drew closer. "Dunno. Sometimes Miguel reckons he sees things, and I'm not sure if he's had too many beans or if he really is."

"Are you telling me we've had trespassers? Why didn't I know about this? Where? When?"

"Boss, it's Miguel. I'm not sure if the man is on drugs half the time but he's not always seeing what's really there, if you know what I mean."

"Whoa. Did you just say Miguel is on drugs? You know we have a drug-free policy here. I can't believe—"

"Boss, come on. How long have I been working here? Longer than you."

Jackson rubbed the back of his head. Denny had taken on the role a year or so after his father had left. "I don't mean to sound disrespectful. But we've always been cautious about who we employ."

"Miguel is not on drugs. Once upon a time, probably. And that's likely the reason he gets hallucinations."

"We've got hallucinations going on now?"

"No. Not all the time. Not at all. Except for the times he thinks he's seen some man."

"And do you think it's true?"

"It's Miguel. He thinks every sage bush is a coyote."

"Then why do we employ him?"

"Because he's cheap, and he's good with the horses."

But was that enough for him to stay? Jackson was all about second chances—and fourth and fifth chances—but there was something unsettling about learning this about an employee. And to learn his foreman had kept such news from him, and it had taken a midnight barn visit for the truth to come out.

"I can't believe it's taken until now for you to tell me."

"Sorry, boss."

Jackson scrubbed his eyes. Coming to the barn hadn't exactly been the reprieve from anxious thoughts that he'd hoped for.

He gave Brutus a final scratch on the head and followed Denny in locking up the barn, but he was still too restless to sleep. Thoughts still cluttered his mind worse than the papers cluttering his desk. He moved to the metal gate that led down to the cattle yard. A coyote's yip echoed on the cool night air. As his eyes adjusted, he saw the outline of small hills and valleys, the legacy of Great-grandfather Reilly measured in every tree and blade of grass. He exhaled and hung his arms over the cold iron as a few faint stars above lit the darkness with ancient promise.

What was it Lexi's dad had said in his sermon? Something about being grateful, choosing to be thankful for all things, even in the midst of turmoil and confusion. Maybe it was time to practice what had been preached.

So he thanked God for His favor. Thanked God for his family. Thanked God for his mom. His friends. For Lexi. For his health. For the ranch. For Denny. Miguel. Brutus. Fido. Food. A house. Clothing. A bed.

And thanked God that He knew what He was doing, and His faithfulness meant Jackson could let go of his worries and trust Him.

CHAPTER TWELVE

"Oh, Lexi darling. How are you?"

Her mother smothered her in a hug as the morning congregation filed past them to go inside. What had her mother thought might happen at the Reilly ranch?

"I'm fine, Mum." Well, truth be told, she was also a little flustered still by Jackson, especially after that unnerving encounter two nights ago.

When he'd come in for breakfast yesterday morning—he'd apparently slept in the bunkhouse, which was strange—he'd seemed a little more at peace, meeting her eyes and offering her a smile that made her heart kick. Fluster didn't even begin to cover it, but she'd done her best to hide it from Ellie. She suspected Jackson's sister wasn't fooled.

"Are you sure?" Mum's voice lowered. "Is everything okay with that young man?"

"Do you mean Jackson?"

"Of course! Why? How many other young men are there?"

Lexi didn't figure her mother needed to know about the ranch hands. "Honestly, Mum, he's fine. Everything is fine. I'm safe, I have my own room, and he's not even in the main house."

"No?"

"He stayed in the bunkhouse, Mum, so you don't need to worry."

"Well, that is good to hear."

"I don't know what you thought might happen."

"Darling, you need to know it's part of a mother's lot to worry." Her mother's eyes slipped below Lexi's chin where a scarf again hid her scar.

Okay, so perhaps she could understand. Nevertheless. "You don't need to," Lexi said firmly. "I'm having fun."

"You're not working too hard?"

"Just hard enough." Who knew tidying and cleaning up a ranch house could be fun? Then last night, having a barbecue as they watched the sun go down, something even Mrs. Reilly had managed to come out and enjoy. Her heart had been full, watching the gladness lining Ellie and Jackson's faces as the family quietly interacted. "It's so pretty out there. You should come visit some time."

"Hmm."

"I think you'd like it. The hills are beautiful and peaceful, and sometimes you can hear wolves call."

"There are wolves?" Her mother's eyes doubled in size.

"No." God forgive her that evasion. "Not on the Reilly's land. And honestly, Mum, the thing you should be focused on is Mrs. Reilly, and the fact that she's doing better."

"Well, I suppose that is good to hear."

She *supposed*? Her disbelief must've shown on her face, for her mother patted her arm. "I'm glad to hear you're okay. Now, you do have the whole day off? Can you come to lunch like I messaged?"

"I'd like to," she said slowly. Mrs. Reilly was being looked after by a respite carer, which had freed Lexi from her duties today. She'd been looking forward to spending time with her parents, but also wanted to spend time with some of the other younger people Ellie had mentioned.

"But you have made other plans?" her mother guessed. "If you have, that's perfectly okay. I just wanted to spend some time with you."

There it was again, the tug of familial obligation. "I'll be there."

"You sure? I don't want to interrupt your plans."

"They weren't set in concrete." She shrugged. "Ellie mentioned going to the diner with some of the others, and—"

"She can come too. And your young man."

"He's not my young man, Mum."

Her mother's gaze halted, then lifted to somewhere above Lexi's shoulder. Awesome. One guess who that was.

"Good morning, Mrs. Franklin." Jackson's drawl made every hair stand up. Or perhaps that was his nearness. She could feel the heat of his presence as he moved beside her.

"Jackson." Her mother's face and tone held friendliness, but Lexi could still see the tension in her eyes. "How is your mother?"

"Doing a lot better since your daughter came on the scene."

Her mother shot Lexi a proud smile. "She's always been so compassionate."

"And patient. And merciful."

Her heart clenched as she got the sense he was now referring to how she'd treated him. She glanced up at him. He was looking down at her, and the tweak of his lips suggested he liked what he saw.

"Ahem." Her mother's cleared throat snapped her gaze away. "Lexi, if you would like to invite some friends to join us for lunch, please know that they are very welcome."

"Thanks." No time like the present. "Would you like to come, Jackson?"

"Uh, sure." He shot her mother a look. "I can see if Ellie is free."

"If you can get her away from Jasper." Lexi studied the pair, who were talking near the church steps.

He frowned. "Those two have always been thick as thieves."

"He can come as well. The more the merrier, they always say." Mum nodded to Jackson with a smile that held a little more genuineness than Lexi had expected. She patted Lexi on the shoulder, then moved to talk to some other congregation members.

"Is that okay?" Lexi asked. "I know you probably had other plans."

"I wouldn't have said yes if I hadn't meant it," he said.

Honestly, a girl could drown in the liquid chocolate depths of his eyes. She straightened, aiming for cool. "Look at me, the wild and crazy gal who has lunch with her parents."

"I'm glad for the chance to get to know them," he said, sincerity in his voice. Of course. He had no dad and his mother wasn't well, so a family lunch might be something he viewed as a privilege, not a chore. Remorse kneaded at how she'd regarded the invitation.

"I'll go ask Ellie," Jackson said, offering her a smile before turning on his booted heel.

The service began not long after, and Lexi couldn't help but be aware of eyes looking their way. Of course, that might have been because Jackson had chosen to sit next to her and his height and breadth of shoulders meant he wasn't easy to miss. And while she hoped the attention stemmed from her experience with Jordan—who was back in church again—she couldn't help but think there was another reason for why so many people were watching her today. She touched the scarf. It was still in place. Jackson looked at her, and the knowledge that he'd seen what she had tried to hide for so long again brought back the same shimmery feeling of vulnerability as that first night. A rawness. Something that tipped her insides up then down, mingling with the strangest feeling of relief.

Jackson shifted, his right hand wrapping around the edge of the wooden pew, mere millimeters from hers.

She barely heard Pastor Ladan's talk, conscious of Jackson's hand so close to hers. Did he feel as though sparks arced between them? But what could be the point of pursuing a relationship with him, especially if she returned to Australia? Anyway, he'd told his brothers he didn't feel that way about her. She couldn't let him mess with her heart. She closed her eyes, not willing to shift a muscle.

Lord, I don't know what this is, but please protect my heart. I don't want to lose it to a handsome cowboy who will lead me astray.

"You okay?" he whispered.

Lexi opened her eyes and nodded, directing her attention to the front.

But try as she might, she couldn't stop the flurry of sensation that simply being near him induced. Even breathing only seemed to draw attention to his delicious scent, a heady mix of moss and leather that made her stomach coil.

Somehow she sang the last song and managed to smile and make small talk with Barb and her friends as they waited to exit. But that was only on the surface. Deep down, it was like her very bones and marrow responded to Jackson's briefest touch. His hand on the small of her back as he guided her forward. His arm brushing hers as they passed down the front steps. His breath dancing along her face as he bent to hear her voice. He was attentive and considerate, more considerate than any man she'd ever been out with. Not that she'd been out with many. Her studies and workload and Christian faith requirements had meant past boyfriends could be counted on three fingers. Not that she was thinking of Jackson as boyfriend material. But apparently, judging from some of the knowing glances being shot her way, perhaps she should.

"Ah, Jackson." The realtor man—Bob?—drew near, a large lady dressed in flounces in an unflattering shade of pink by his side. He nodded to Lexi, but the woman's eyes rounded as she saw how close Jackson stood to Lexi.

Lexi offered a small smile and subtly shifted, putting a good couple of inches between them. "Good morning."

"Oh, it is." The woman smiled as the two men started talking. "I'm Rhonda Ingalls."

"Lexi Franklin."

"Ah, that's right. I hear you're staying at the Reilly ranch."

"Yes."

The woman glanced at Jackson and back at Lexi, raising her eyebrows, her insinuation clear.

Lexi's hackles rose. Was this the woman Ellie had mentioned? "Did you also hear that I'm caring for Mrs. Reilly?"

"No, I didn't know. Is there something wrong with her? Oh my!"

Lexi gritted her teeth. Judging from the abrupt halt to the men's conversation and the concerned look Jackson shot her, that had been the wrong thing to say. "Please excuse me."

She mouthed a "sorry" at Jackson and moved away, weaving around bodies until she reached Ellie, who was talking with Jasper. "Are you ready to go?"

"Sure." Ellie glanced at Jasper. "You're happy to tag along, aren't you?"

He nodded.

"I'll head there with Jasper. You can go with Jackson."

Her cheeks heated. "I guess."

But add fuel to the fire of speculation by leaving church together? Maybe it'd be easier to dampen some flames. She found Jackson and told him she'd see him at the Bible College, and hitched a ride with her parents instead.

———

JACKSON TOYED with his water glass, the conversation leaving him a little more unsettled. Or maybe that was because Lexi had chosen not to ride here with him. He could've sworn she felt the same sparks before, and from the way she looked at him, he'd thought she felt the same heat as he did. But then she'd travelled here with her parents, like she didn't want to be with him. Which was probably understandable. Lexi was close with her family—anyone could see that—and he kinda wished he'd been privileged to grow up with the hugs and easy affection he saw between Lexi and her parents. He couldn't blame her for wanting more of that. The ranch could never offer a simple life, although he'd caught a glimpse of that ease last night, watching the sun set, pooling gold across the hills and in Lexi's hair. He could've stayed there with her forever.

He glanced at her now. Her gaze remained averted, her chin propped on one hand as her elbow rested on the table. Not something his mom would've approved of.

His smile faded as Lexi's mom studied him, a small furrow in her brow, like she wasn't sure what to make of him. That was fair, because he didn't know what to make of her either. He couldn't blame a mom for wanting the best for her daughter. And Jackson wasn't that, not with more baggage than Spokane Airport.

Jasper was talking, and Jackson forced a smile in Mrs. Franklin's direction, then turned to tune into the conversation. He'd never noticed before, but Jasper seemed to light up around his sister. Weird. He'd always considered Jasper more his friend than Ellie's. Apparently Jackson's focus on the ranch had stolen his attention from other things.

"And what about you, Ellie?" Mrs. Franklin asked. "I understand you're interested in studying history?"

"I was, but ranch life takes a fair bit of time," his sister said.

"She wants to travel and see museums," Lexi said.

She did? He shot Ellie a look.

She shrugged. "Maybe one day."

Regret streaked across Jackson's chest. If only his work didn't demand his sister's hours too, then he'd gladly see her off to have adventures around the world. Judging from the way Jasper was looking at her, with a warmth that kinda shocked him, the sooner he could get her away from here to explore her options, the better.

He stole another glance at Lexi, then found her mother studying him again too.

He managed a weak smile as he played with the cake crumbs on his plate. Maybe Mrs. Franklin felt the same sense of protectiveness for her daughter as he felt for Ellie. Which was completely understandable, given Lexi had undergone such trauma. He couldn't blame her mom for wanting Lexi to have options, to have the best. Which he clearly wasn't.

The conversation moved on as Mr. Franklin talked about the upcoming influx of summer students, and the work that still needed to be done, including fixing the driveway. Was Mr. Franklin's comment a hint that Jackson having taken Lexi away had deprived them of extra hands? Lexi had proved herself capable at the ranch, but Jackson didn't figure she'd be up for fixing roads.

"I could maybe grade that road for you," he said to Mr. Franklin.

Lexi's dad studied him, as if he recognized Jackson's offer as the pathetic plea to accept Jackson that it was. Getting in the good books, however he could. "I wouldn't want to take you away from your duties now, son."

"I'd be happy to help," he said, with less certainty.

Lexi glanced at him now, as if recognizing his withering resolve, and she sent him a quick smile that put fresh air in his hopes.

"Peter, you've been complaining about that road for months, so let the young man help you." Mrs. Franklin sent him a warm smile much like her daughter's. "Honestly. What is it about men that means they're never able to accept help?"

"I don't know," Lexi said, her gaze not leaving Jackson. "Is it that they don't like to appear weak?"

"You don't think Jackson is weak, do you Lexi?" Ellie said, with a wink for him.

His ears burned, and Lexi's face pinked.

Jasper reached across and slapped him on the back. "Strongest man in the wrestling team, three years running."

"Last decade," Jackson muttered.

"I don't know if you've seen our other teammates lately, but it's safe to assume you're still the strongest," Jasper said dryly.

"You did wrestling?" Lexi studied him with an expression of fascination.

"Just at school." It had been a way to prove he fit in, and a much cheaper and easier sport for his mom to manage than the hockey Mitchell had always insisted on. And look how well that worked out for him. Jackson's debts and failures meant he'd never fit in.

He played with the edge of his plate, rubbing his finger back and forth along the silver rim. Maybe that's how life worked. Maybe nice guys really did come last. He'd put others first and look where that got him. Busting his guts for years, and for what? A broken ranch and broken dreams. He blinked hard against the self-pity, and with effort forced himself to meet his hosts' gazes.

His hosts, who lived here in this fancy building with their much-loved daughter, who only deserved the best. He forced an edge of his mouth up, hoping it counted as a smile, and hid the despair gnawing within.

"Jackson, tell me about the ranch," Peter Franklin said. "What do you actually do there? I have to confess I've always been more of a town man, so I'm not familiar with what goes on."

Somehow Jackson relaxed enough to share about his hopes

and goals. He confessed Brutus's failure as a stud, and how this had put a hole in their plans. He glanced apologetically at Ellie, whose smile of sympathy made him feel a little better.

"I've been praying for him," Lexi said.

"Who?" her mother asked.

"Brutus," Lexi said, gazing at him.

His heart softened, then softened some more as Ellie said, "I have too."

"It appears we'll all have to pray for Brutus," Peter Franklin said.

"Indeed," Mrs. Franklin said, her expression one of sympathy.

He swallowed a lump, managing to rasp out, "Appreciate it." The conversation moved to Ellie's invitation for Lexi's parents to come visit the ranch, and he was grateful for the change in subject.

Mr. and Mrs. Franklin glanced at each other, then at him, then at Ellie. "Lexi said we should," Mrs. Franklin said. "She says it's beautiful."

"You said that?" he blurted.

"Of course. Because it *is* beautiful. And so peaceful. I love it there."

She might have missed it, but Jackson caught the way her parents looked at each other again, with that "uh oh" look that he'd seen other parents wear.

But their concerns didn't matter, as Lexi's words had buoyed his spirits. "I couldn't imagine living anywhere else."

Maybe he said that with more force than he'd intended, for her gaze dropped, and it became her turn to investigate her plate. And while he meant his words, he also knew he might have to. The bank's deadline for alternative arrangements was drawing closer, and he remained as clueless as ever about what to do. But somehow, deeper within, he felt a strong conviction that God would work things out. God had provided for his mother, by placing the angel that was Lexi in the Reilly household. Surely God would provide a way for them to stay on the ranch.

"You know, I think the ranch would make a great farm stay," Lexi said.

"A what?" Jasper asked.

"Ooh, yes," Ellie said. "Our ranch is beautiful. I might be biased, but I think it's got a much nicer outlook than the Darcy's ranch next door. They apparently wanted to buy the property from Granddad, but he refused to sell any Reilly land." This was said with a stern look in Jackson's direction. "But I think people would love to come and stay. And it could provide some extra income."

"But what would people do?" Jasper asked.

"Come on, Jasper. Use your imagination. They could ride horses, swim in the river, collect eggs, read books, watch movies, eat outside, and watch the sunset."

"And you already have the bunkhouse accommodation," Lexi said. "I think people would love to come."

Ellie frowned. "We'd have to tidy up a few things."

Mr. Franklin nodded, as if he too had caught the enthusiasm rippling around the dining table. "Superficial improvements should be easily managed. As long as it doesn't steal too much focus from your usual routines."

"You'd just need a way of letting people know," Lexi said.

"That's easy," Ellie said. "Dermott, my oldest brother, his wife Mindy is great at social media. We could ask her for some ideas. I bet she'd know how we could market the place to attract visitors."

"Or you could ask Tabby Thomas at the Lakeside Inn," Mrs. Franklin said. "I understand they're fully booked until Memorial Day, so she must know something about attracting guests."

"Wait." This was getting out of control. "Mr. Franklin is right. This might be a great idea, but I don't have time to devote to this. I barely have enough hours in the day to sleep, let alone entertain visitors. We'd need someone who'd be happy to do that. And we can't afford to pay more staff."

The table fell silent for a few moments. He glanced out the window, catching a glimpse of Wainscott Lake.

"How many extra staff would you need?" Mrs. Franklin said. "If you make things fairly self-sufficient, like provide breakfast baskets, and don't provide meals, then perhaps you could still make things work." She held up her hands apologetically. "Of course, I'm no expert, but I have helped run this place for many years. Once you work out the logistics and your systems and can encourage people to look after themselves as much as possible, then things become much more doable."

Hope fluttered around the corners of his chest. "It's something, but it wouldn't be enough." Definitely not something enough by the time the bank demanded payment.

"I think it's a great idea," Ellie said. "I think we should talk to Mom and do it."

"Is your father not around?" Mrs. Franklin asked.

How to kill the mood with one question. "He left when I was a boy."

"I was a baby," Ellie said. "I don't remember him at all."

"I'm so sorry," Lexi's mom murmured.

Ellie shrugged, but her face was hard. "He made it clear he wanted nothing to do with us, and we're happy for it to stay that way. I don't even know what I'd say to him if he appeared."

"Surely he wouldn't, not after so many years," Jasper said. "Wasn't he declared legally dead?"

Ellie nodded, her lips flat.

"Mom needed to do that in order to keep the ranch running," Jackson said. "She spent years trying to raise us and keep the ranch afloat, but it's worn her down. I took it on years ago, and have power of attorney, but it's hard work." He cleared his throat. "That's why it's such a blessing to have Lexi there to care for Mom when she gave so much of herself to us."

There was a beat or two of silence. He tried to smile at Lexi, but her look of intense sympathy made him swallow again.

"Your mother will be in our prayers, as well," Peter Franklin assured.

And from the nod of approval being sent his way, Jackson knew he would be as well.

CHAPTER THIRTEEN

"Oh, my word. It really is as pretty as you said," Lexi's mother said, hands propped on a wooden fence post as she gazed across the Reilly ranch. This was fast becoming Lexi's favorite time of day, when the first soft pinks of sunset settled over the furrows of hills and valleys like a goodnight kiss.

This evening had proved the only time her parents could manage before the Bible College's summer session began in two days' time. After Ellie had practically begged them at lunch on Sunday to come visit, they had finally agreed.

"It's so peaceful, isn't it?" Lexi said, watching a bird ascend in poetic flight.

"I can understand why you like it here. It's not exactly the big smoke, is it?"

"Not exactly." Not at all.

"I think it could make a wonderful vacation spot for tourists."

Jackson had taken them on a quick tour earlier, and they'd seen the bunkhouses, which her parents agreed made for unexpectedly good accommodation. "A good dusting and a lick of paint is all these rooms need."

"Exactly," her mother had said. "I think it holds a rustic charm that would prove most appealing for city dwellers."

Ellie had called another family meeting after Sunday lunch and put the idea of a farm stay to her brothers. Lexi hadn't been privy to the conversation but knew Ellie had been disappointed with Cooper and Mitchell's doubts, even though Dermott had seemed on board. "I don't understand why they can complain when Mom is happy about it."

"Happy" might be something of an overstatement, but Lexi had been there when Jackson and Ellie had broached the idea, and she hadn't said no. Not that it would matter, given Jackson had power of attorney. She figured that meant he was ultimately responsible for what happened. Lexi had also been there when Ellie messaged Mindy, Dermott's wife, who had offered ideas on how to progress via social media platforms. So maybe this idea could have legs. As it should. Who wouldn't want to spend time in an idyllic place like this?

She drew in a deep breath of mild summer evening air, catching the tang of browning meat. Jackson was cooking the barbecue he'd promised and they were eating outside, even though Ellie had complained the mosquitoes were sure to be out and ready to feast too. But when Mrs. Reilly had indicated she'd be happy to eat outside, all arguments died. She might be still unwell, but the fact she'd seemed happier, and had made more visits out of her room in recent days was encouraging.

"I'll check on Mrs. Reilly." Lexi turned to move away.

"Jackson was right," Mum said.

She paused. "In what way?"

"You are a blessing to this family. To his mother. To him."

Heat danced up her cheeks. "I'm just doing what I'm trained to do."

"Are you sure about this?"

"Being here?"

"Oh, I understand now why you enjoy working here." Her

mother's glance lifted to where Jackson stood, talking with Dad and Jasper, the three men bonding over grilled meat the way men seemed to bond the world over.

"Mum."

"Lexi." Her mother smiled. "He's a nice man. But no, that wasn't what I meant. Well, it wasn't all I meant. Are you sure about transferring your qualifications over here?"

Ah, the conversation they'd had in the car between church and the Bible college last weekend. "I want a different scene, a different pace. And it's not just about the attack, Mum." Her hand drifted to her throat. She'd forgone the scarf for the first time today. Everyone here had seen her without it now, so trying to hide her scar seemed silly. "Double shifts are killers, and I know I don't want to do that anymore." Working sixteen hours straight? No, thanks. "I want a life. I feel like I could have one in a small town like this."

"Have you made enquiries about work placements?"

"There's a lot to sort out before I can think about that," Lexi said. "But there's the hospital in Trinity Lakes, and other clinics nearby. I'm sure I could get work. But I don't need it right now."

"But you'll need money soon," her mother said. "Your savings won't last forever."

"I've barely touched my savings. Being here on the ranch means I've hardly spent a dime."

Her mother smiled. "Look at you, talking American."

"It's probably inevitable if I'm going to stay here."

Her mother nodded. "If you're sure."

Lexi offered a strained smile and she murmured something about getting the salads. She moved closer to where Ellie and Mrs. Reilly sat in deck chairs, watching the sky tint rose and gold. Ellie grinned as she held her mother's hand.

Jackson flipped meat patties, and Lexi marveled at how easily he seemed to be getting on with her father. Judging from her mother's pre-church comments, she wasn't sure what her parents thought of the cowboy, but he seemed to have won them over during lunch. Or maybe it was the fact he'd headed to the Bible College yesterday and graded their driveway as promised.

Jackson met her gaze and winked, and she retreated to the kitchen. She braced her hands on either side of the sink and drew in a breath. Where was this going? Was she letting herself fall into heartbreak? It wasn't like Jackson had said or done anything apart from exchange a few too-long glances with her. She exhaled, shoulders lowering. Maybe this wasn't something to pin such dramatic life choices on. And she didn't really want to do that, to make decisions based on a man. But she couldn't help the sparkles that lit inside whenever he smiled at her. "Lord," she whispered. "I could really do with knowing if he feels the same way too."

A noise from the front drive, the crunch of wheels on pebbles, drew her attention. Who was here? Jackson had released the ranch hands to have a night off in town, and they weren't expected to finish the meal and movie until much later.

She wandered down the hall and peered through the glass pane in the upper part of the front door. Her eyes widened. Who drove a convertible around here? Maybe the man was lost and looking for the fancy Darcy estate next door.

She opened the door and moved onto the front porch and saw the car's California plates. Then she recognized the man from photos she'd seen inside.

"You must be Cooper."

"Call me Coop," he said, brown eyes twinkling. "And you're pretty."

"Actually, I'm Lexi. Lexi Franklin."

He nodded, his gaze dipping below her chin to her throat then straight back up again, with none of the eye-widening or gasps of horror she'd come to expect. "Jackson's pretty nurse?"

"Your mum's, actually."

He chuckled, and again she felt a tug of easy appeal with this family. He swung a bag from his car—so he'd be staying—and then ascended the steps of the porch, gesturing for her to enter the house before him. He followed her through the hall, muttering "the place is looking better"—yes, it did, thanks to her hard work—then dropped his bag in the hall.

"You plan to stay a while?"

"For a few days, at least. Long enough to see this latest crazy scheme that my brother is trying."

"What he's trying to do is to save the ranch."

"Hmm." He studied her a moment and she wasn't sure what he saw. "How's Mom?"

"Doing better." She gestured through the glass doors to outside. "She's outside at the moment. She's been feeling stronger, so she's making the most of this nice weather."

He nodded, tilting his head to the other car in the yard. "Someone else is here?"

"Jasper. And my parents."

"Your parents?" Again that glimmer of amusement. "So you and Jackson—"

"Are friends," she said coolly, even though the more time she spent in his company, the more she wanted more. Jackson might be under pressure, but he was also kind and compassionate, and she liked him.

"Okay." His look of amusement said *sure, whatever you say.* "Ellie around?"

"She's out the back with your mum."

"Mum?" He grinned. "I like it."

"Excuse me while I get some salads."

"Need help?"

"Uh, sure. If you can grab some plates from there." She pointed to the cupboards, then felt foolish. He used to live here. He'd know where the plates were.

"How many?"

"Seven, no eight if you're eating with us."

"If there's enough food."

"I think your brother planned to feed an army. You'll be fine."

She grabbed the bowls of potato salad and coleslaw, resting a plate of bread rolls on top, and moved outside in time to catch the wave of "Cooper" as the second-youngest Reilly made his appearance.

The next hour passed in food and laughter as the Reillys caught up. Mrs. Reilly had a glow about her that Lexi hadn't seen before. Perhaps she truly was on the mend.

"You're blessed to have grown up here," Lexi's father said. "I bet you can see all the stars at night."

"So many," Ellie said.

"My grandfather was into astronomy. I think I still have his telescope somewhere," Cooper said. "You're welcome to check it out if you're here in a few hours."

Dessert was delayed as Jackson made the most of the dying light to give his brother a quick tour of the premises, which naturally saw the rest of them join in. Cooper helped his mother as she took shaky steps.

"She's doing so well," Lexi overheard Ellie murmur to Jasper.

"Good nurse, huh?"

"The best." Ellie smiled at Lexi, her gaze shifting beyond her shoulder. "Wouldn't you agree, Jackson? Lexi is the best?"

"Sure is."

His deep look sent a tingle all through her, and she was glad for the dimness as they entered the barn.

"So this is the famous Brutus," Cooper said, looking at the bull. "He sure doesn't look like he's unhappy."

"How could he be with all these beautiful women staring at him?" Jasper said, which earned Ellie's elbow. "What?"

Lexi inched closer to the pen, inadvertently brushing past Jackson, and she wobbled. Then, in a move reminiscent of their first encounter, he swooped an arm around her and drew her close, so she was pressed against his chest.

"Ooh, look who has all the moves," Ellie murmured.

Lexi pushed away from him, knowing her cheeks were bright red.

"We had a New Year's Eve party here," Ellie continued, speaking to Lexi's parents as if she hadn't just embarrassed Lexi and Jackson, whose cheeks looked as hot as hers felt.

"It was really fun," Jasper said.

"Sure was." Ellie showed Lexi's mother her phone and scrolled through pictures.

"Well, that is pretty," Mum said. "It's hard to believe a barn could be transformed."

"We don't let first impressions last, do we, Jackson?"

"No."

"Coop may, but hey, he's never been as smart as some of us," Ellie teased.

"Yeah. Right." Cooper rolled his eyes.

"You know what? I feel like we should show 'em how it's done. C'mon, Jasp."

As the banjo-like introduction of one of Keith Urban's most famous songs came through Ellie's phone, she grabbed Jasper's hands and drew him into a waltz hold.

"Go on, Jackson. Ask Lexi to dance."

He glanced at her and held out his hands. She grasped them and he pulled her close, placing an arm around her back as he lightly held her right hand. From the corner of her eyes she caught her parents smiling, then they too shuffled into a dance pose. Then they were moving, and all awareness of other things slipped away as Jackson's height and breadth drew her head up. But it was the intensity of his gaze that meant she couldn't look away. His lips quirked up at both ends, his smile holding a promise she wanted to explore. He swung her around as Keith sang in the background about wanting to love somebody—

"Like you," Jackson murmured.

Her chest fluttered. Surely he didn't mean that?

She grew vaguely aware of clapping and whistles, and comments—from whom, she couldn't discern, focused as she was on the man who held her in his arms. He was smiling, his smile tearing all embarrassment away. He softly sang along, his eyes intent on her, and she was helpless to do anything but follow along.

Breath suspended as she sank deeper into his hold, his lips mouthing the chorus again.

The singing cut away and he pulled her close, and she closed her eyes as he swayed with her for a few precious more moments. Was this something of an answer to prayer? *Lord?*

As if in answer, Jackson's clasp tightened on hers, and the banjo started again. She grew aware they had an audience, and pasted a smile over her flustered feelings as Jackson spun her around one more time to the final chorus filtering through the phone.

Then he paused, chest heaving as he clasped her in a move similar to their classic hold from before, except this time it held intention, as his face was close to hers, a breath away from kissing her.

"Whew." Cooper said. "It's getting warm in here."

Jackson's mouth ticked up a fraction more on one side, then he pulled her upright.

Lexi fanned herself. "I think I need a cool drink. It's been a long time since I've danced."

Ellie wore a smug expression, as did Jasper. Even Mrs. Reilly seemed to have enjoyed the show.

"How about if I go see if those desserts are ready?" Mrs. Reilly's words led to a general exodus from the barn, apart from Jackson who continued studying Lexi as if she was a treasure map to a gold mine.

"What is it?" she asked softly.

He opened his mouth, but before he could speak, Cooper's voice sang from the door, "You two coming?"

"I guess that's our cue," Jackson said.

That was all? She nodded, disappointment crowding her chest as she followed him from the barn.

———

THE NIGHT SKY gleamed with a diamond spray of stars. They'd finished dessert, and Jasper had gone home while Lexi was settling his mom into bed. Mr. Franklin—Peter—and Lynette planned to leave soon too, having had a quick look at the stars through Coop's newly found telescope.

"The sky is so beautiful," Peter said.

"We might not be officially classified as Big Sky country, but I like to think the view here is as good as anything you'll see in Montana."

"Being perched up higher on a hill you really get great vistas."

"Yeah." Earlier he'd pointed out where the Darcy solar farm bordered their fence line. "When Liam Darcy wanted to build his solar farm, I asked that they build it to project their lights downward so we can enjoy the night sky. They did, but then, he's a good neighbor."

"It's important to love your neighbors," Ellie had said, her waggling eyebrows letting him know exactly which neighbor he should be focused on. The one he'd been singing to as Keith Urban sang all that was in Jackson's heart. The one who was again helping his mom, and who had withdrawn into shyness since their impromptu dance an hour or so ago.

"True," Peter said. "I wonder if you could offer night sky viewing as one of your attractions when you open up for accommodation."

"That would be wonderful. Supper under the stars, like we're doing now," Lynette Franklin said.

"Supper under the stars, I like it. Sounds romantic." Ellie had glanced at Jackson. "What do you think? Do you know enough about stars to sound like you know what you're talking about?"

"It's not hard," Coop said, like he thought his big brother was dumb.

And maybe he was the dumbest cowboy in the world, taking advice from greenhorns. But the fact they all—except maybe Coop—seemed to believe this venture could work made him believe it too, had led him to work out a business plan with Jasper earlier in the day. He'd get the math-minded Cooper to look over the plan before he submitted it to the bank later this week. Hope lit his heart, daring him to believe that all kinds of things might have a chance at working out.

"Jackson?"

"Oh, uh, yeah. Sure."

"Mmm. Real convincing," Ellie said. "But we might be able to pull it off, if there's anyone here who knows what they're talking about." She toed Coop's fancy Italian leather boot, which had obviously never seen a hard day's work.

"You talking about me?" Coop said. "No way. I have a job."

"You also have a family."

"I could see what my schedule is like," Peter said. "Assuming you'd like to have an Aussie pointing out American stars."

"Really?"

"I admire your initiative, and think it'd be fun to be with other star buffs. I find I sometimes need an excuse to get out of the Bible school bubble and mix with real people."

"Happy to oblige, sir. Of course, this is all dependent on how things go at the bank."

"Well, you have my number. If I can help at all, let me know. And I meant what I said before. If you need some willing workers to get those bunkhouses painted, I'll have students looking to volunteer for those kinds of jobs as part of the community component of their course. If you're interested, let me know as soon as possible so I can set that up."

"I'll say yes, then. Thank you, sir."

They set a time, then Lexi's parents rose, thanked them for the evening, and moved back to the house just as Lexi came out.

"Oh, I'm glad I didn't miss saying goodbye."

"Is Mom okay?" he asked.

"She's fine. Just took a little while to settle, probably because she's not used to all this excitement."

"None of us are," Jackson said.

Her gaze slid to her parents, and the next minute was spent in hugs and goodbyes and thanks, things that made him long for such open affection.

Peter Franklin held out his hand and Jackson shook it. "Thanks again, sir. You've really been generous."

"You reap what you sow, Jackson." He tilted his head to his daughter. "Just take care there, okay?"

"Absolutely, sir. Always."

Peter eyed him a long moment then nodded, and Jackson's heart expanded like a hot air balloon.

He stood on the porch, lifting a hand in farewell as Lexi waved goodbye.

"Thanks so much," she said, her eyes shining. "It was great to be able to show them where I live." She seemed to catch herself saying that. "I mean, where you live, and—"

"I know what you mean." The fact she thought of his place as hers strummed a joyful banjo sound in his heart more powerful than anything in a famous country song.

He reached down, grasped her hand in his. "Want to watch the stars with me?"

He heard her breath catch, and she glanced at their hands, before her gaze slowly trickled back up to his again. "I'm not sure."

"They're really beautiful tonight."

"But your mum—"

"Is asleep, right?"

She nodded, and wet her bottom lip, and he once again felt that urge to press his mouth to hers. Good thing the others had been witnessing their dance before, otherwise he would've tried it then.

"Come on."

He locked the front door and led her through the quiet house, and back outside. They found his younger brother and sister near the remains from dessert, their words quiet as the flames crackled in a steel drum Jackson had repurposed as a fire pit. Not fancy, not finished, like him.

Lexi let go of his fingers and settled into a deckchair next to Ellie. He dragged one to Lexi's other side, close enough to hold her hand if she got over being shy. Because after their dance, it was obvious to all that their attraction was mutual. And yeah, maybe he didn't have all the answers, but the night felt full of possibilities.

"Tonight has been so much fun," Ellie said, dreamily.

"The best." Jackson reached over and threaded his fingers through Lexi's. She startled, and glanced across, and he could see the questions in her eyes. Questions he'd be dealing with as soon as his siblings went to bed. Which reminded him. "Hey, Coop. How long are you planning on staying?"

"A few days."

"You know you'll be staying in the bunkhouse with me, don't you?"

"What? Why?"

Jackson gently squeezed Lexi's fingers. "Because I as good as promised Lexi's parents there'd be no unmarried men staying in the house while she's here."

"Are you serious? My bed is in the house."

"If it's too much trouble I can always stay in the bunkhouse,"

Lexi said quietly.

"No way," Jackson said.

"Nope. Mom needs you nearby," Ellie said.

And the ranch hands certainly didn't need a pretty young woman sleeping alone next to them. "Coop, if you're planning to stay here, then you'll need to bunk down out here with me," Jackson said firmly. "Come on. It'll be like old times."

"We never had old times like that," Coop protested. "Not that I can remember, anyway."

"Don't you remember Granddad used to let us stay out some nights, back when we were small, and pretend to be the ranch hands?"

"Nope. I blotted that from my mind."

"How old were you?" Lexi asked Jackson.

"Maybe five."

"And you want me to remember when I was three?" Coop scoffed. "Look, I'm sorry Lexi, but I drove a long way today, and the one thing keeping me going was thoughts of my bed. I really don't understand what anyone thinks I might do."

"It's not about what you might do," Ellie said. "It's about what others might say."

"Like who?"

"Just … others."

"Who's gonna know?"

Good question.

But judging from the way Lexi slid her hand from Jackson's and shifted in her seat, she held her own reservations. "I think what they're trying to say is that Jackson doesn't want anyone at church thinking he's stashed a girlfriend in his house," she said quietly.

"It's easier to say there was nothing going on when we know it never looked that way," Jackson said. "That's why I've been staying in the bunkhouse since she came."

"Wait. I didn't think you two were …" Coop's voice faded

into the night. "Are you?"

Given the uncertainty Jackson felt now, he wasn't about to make this easy on his brother. "Are we what?"

"Together?" Coop finally asked. Jackson sensed Ellie's gaze, her nose sure to be quivering as much as any fox scenting prey.

There was a beat, then Lexi cleared her throat. "No."

"No. Not yet," Jackson added. "But that could change if you two decided to go catch some zzz's."

"I'm not that tired," Coop protested.

Ellie stood. "Oh, I think you are. Come on. Let's get you sorted in the bunkhouse."

"But—"

"G'night, Coop," Jackson called.

"Have fun, you two," Ellie replied, her tone as mischievous as ever.

"I should probably turn in too." Lexi shifted as if to rise.

"Don't go. Please." He grasped her hand. "Sit a little longer?"

"Don't you have to get up early tomorrow?"

"Yeah, but that's nothing new. Having time alone with you like this is."

After a long moment she nodded, then resumed her position in the chair.

He wove her fingers with his, marveling at the texture, the softness something he was fast coming to associate with this remarkable woman.

Night sounds surrounded them, the hoot of an owl, the distant howl of a wolf. The darkness pressed in, allowing space and quiet for thoughts to untangle, revealing truth. And the truth was he was falling in love with this woman. Keith was right. He wanted to love somebody like Lexi. He wanted her to love him too. And while she might have said there was nothing between them, others clearly disagreed. And the fact she let him keep holding her hand suggested she might not be living up to her decree either.

"Did you mean that before?" she whispered.

"What part?"

"The … the part about not yet."

He smiled, and really wished these deck chairs weren't meant for one. "I sure did."

The starlight revealed the ripple of her throat as she swallowed.

He shifted until he could see her more clearly. "Keith is right."

"Keith?"

He nodded. "Since I met you, it's like I can breathe deeper, more fully. I feel like you believe in me, and I …" His throat grew dry. "And I don't often feel like I believe in myself."

"Oh, Jackson."

He tensed. That wasn't pity, was it?

"I know exactly what you mean," she whispered.

His heart eased. That had been compassion. Empathy, for sure. Whatever it was, it emboldened him to speak more honestly still. "Lexi, I don't have much to offer, but I also know I don't want to live with regrets anymore. And I can't help but feel that if I never said anything then that would be a huge mistake."

"Said anything about what?"

Please, Lord. "I … I'd really like to see if maybe there can be an us one day."

"Us?"

He swallowed. "You. And me."

Her eyes blazed into his.

"I think you're special. Unique. Beautiful. So kind. I meant what I said the other day at your parents'. You've been so compassionate and patient and forgiving. I really like you, Lexi. I mean, I *really* like you. And … and I know I've said and done a whole lot of dumb things, but I hope you know you can trust me."

CHAPTER FOURTEEN

Her heart that had been fluttering at his word, at his touch, quietened at those last two words.

Trust me.

She knew if this relationship was to ever have a chance of working—if she ever wanted any relationship to work—then she'd need to let go of her inhibitions and trust again. Trust a man again. Trust *this* man. This man had proved himself loyal and faithful, his compassion and kindness running as deep as what he seemed to see in her. He deserved nothing less than total honesty.

"I do trust you," she said.

"Yeah?"

"Yes," she whispered.

The moment seemed to stretch with weightiness. She knew what he was asking, and she knew it was time to tell him the truth. But even the security provided by the night didn't make this task easier.

From somewhere behind them a light switched on, pooling a small square of yellow on the lawn. Then came the sound of

Ellie and Cooper talking, Fido's whimpers as Cooper shut the door, then Ellie's cheeky "good night" floated across the still night air.

"She's a card," Lexi murmured.

"Yep." But Jackson didn't sound annoyed with his sister, instead sounding rather pleased at his sister's blatant desire to see Lexi end up with him.

Which stirred her heart flutters again.

His fingers gently caressed hers, and her chest grew tight. "So what are your plans, Ms. Franklin?" he asked.

"My plans?"

"Your future plans. I mean, I can hope all I want, but if you're planning to go back to Australia one day, then I don't think I have enough heart in me to let it break."

Oh. He sounded so much more invested in this than she'd realized. Trusting him meant honoring him with the truth. "I …"

His clasp tightened.

"I have been investigating ways of transferring my qualifications so I can practice nursing here."

"Really?"

"Yes."

"That's good to know." His teeth flashed white in the night sky. "Are you saying you like it around here?"

"Yes."

"The countryside, or the people?"

"Both," she murmured.

"Can I ask if that's anyone in particular?" His voice was low.

"You can."

He chuckled, the sound like warm honey to her ears. "Is there any particular cowboy you might like?"

"Maybe."

"Maybe?" He pushed from his chair and moved to crouch in

front of hers, holding her hand as he leaned close. "Or definitely?"

"Definitely."

He grinned again, and her heart took flight. "Can I guess who that cowboy might be?"

"Sure," she whispered.

"I'm gonna guess that cowboy likes to dance."

"And likes songs by a guy called Keith."

"Uh huh." His breath fanned her face. "But what he really likes is a girl called Lexi."

"Alexandra," she whispered.

He pulled back. "That's your real name?"

"Yes."

He studied her a long moment then drew close again, the rasp of his cheek grazing hers before his head tilted and his lips brushed the side of her face. Then he inched back again as her chair creaked. "You know, these seats really aren't working for me."

His statement shocked her to laughter, and she didn't protest as he pulled her up and drew her to a nearby swing chair. It had slightly dew-damp cushions, but she didn't care.

He wrapped an arm around her in a hold so tender it was like he thought she was made of crystal. Then began the slow exploration of her face with his lips, feathering soft kisses along her brow and cheeks and chin before he lingered, a breath away, at her lips.

She tilted her chin, closed her eyes, and met his mouth with hers.

Stars might meet in the heavens, but it seemed they also met in this kiss. She nestled closer, her stomach fluttering, as her hands slid up into his hair, and his arms slid around to hold her more securely. His lips firmed into passion, possessing hers with a reverent fire that branded her soul and claimed her heart as his.

Oh, this cowboy could kiss.

Judging from his sigh and increased ardor he might feel the same about her. Like God might've brought them from opposite corners of the globe to find each other, to fit together, to share a future and a hope. There was magic here, born of starlight and shared breath.

He groaned, and pulled away, his chest pushing in and out. "Wow, Ms. Lexi."

"Wow yourself, cowboy."

They stared at each other for a long, long time. Then he traced a hand down her cheek, before his fingers slipped to her chin, then her throat. And she knew what was coming next.

———

THE SENSATION of soaring through heavenly heights following the best kiss of Jackson's life faded as he felt her stiffen. He lifted his finger from the pink seam decorating her throat, and she shifted slightly, putting cool air between them.

"You don't have to tell me," he murmured.

"I think I do."

She leaned her head against his chest, pulling her knees up on the swing and wrapping her arms around them. He tugged her closer, his arm around her shoulders, his chin resting on the crown of her head.

Then she sighed.

Then began to speak.

"I was working in the hospital emergency department one Friday night at the end of February. It was a fairly ordinary shift, triaging patients according to their needs, like kids with broken bones or small toys stuck up their nose, old people's headaches and shortness of breath—the usual. Then as the night drew on, the end-of-week fun began." She shivered. "The drunks, the people who spent too long in the pub, whose slurred words and vomiting made life fun."

Fun? Queen of irony, sitting right here.

"Some were violent, most were not. But the ones to watch out for were those on harder drugs—heroin, speed, and ice." Her body trembled again, and she nestled deeper into his arms.

"This guy came in. He just looked like the usual drugged-out party dude, except for being a little more handsome than most. At first, he seemed relatively normal. I definitely didn't expect the sudden escalation in his behavior. One minute he was speaking normally, the next he was shouting at an older-looking couple, terrifying a poor old man who'd dared to ask him to stop swearing."

She shook her head, and shifted again, moving her head up closer to his. He pressed a kiss to her forehead.

"I pressed the alarm for security. They're usually never too far away on weekends, but they'd been responding to an incident in Maternity. I found out later a scuffle had broken out between the father of a new baby and the woman's ex."

"Messy family."

"Poor baby." She sighed. "Anyway, security couldn't come, which left me and Doreen—who's in her mid-fifties—to intervene. I did my best to cool things down, but the guy ..." She gulped. "The guy wasn't having a bar of it, wasn't listening to reason."

He saw a tear trickle down her cheek, and he pressed the pad of his thumb to wipe it away. "You don't have to tell me."

"I want to," she said, her voice scarcely more than a whisper. "I couldn't leave the poor people out there. It didn't seem right, no matter what our protocols are. There were people trying to leave, others calling the police, while Doreen kept calling security. So I left the secured area, like the man was screaming at me to do. I thought ... I thought maybe I could calm him down. But before I knew it, he'd grabbed me, and had a knife at my throat."

"Oh, Lexi," he breathed, his pulse hammering loudly in his ears.

"I froze. I knew self-defense, and I've done plenty of training courses. I should've known better, but I just stood there, scared. So, so scared."

He tucked her closer, smoothing her hair, praying for peace.

"The security guards finally came, and he threatened to cut me if they came closer." She drew in a shaky breath and didn't continue.

"And someone came closer."

She dipped her head. "There's something surreal about seeing your own blood slipping through your hands, spilling on the floor."

"Lexi."

"It seemed to shock the guy. I don't think he meant to do it—he was in a drug-induced psychosis—but all I remember was being on the floor, hands on my throat, people screaming, wanting to scream, strangers holding a towel under my chin while I wondered if I'd ever talk again."

"I'm so sorry." He physically hurt for her, like every cell inside him felt her pain.

"What's weird is that I didn't ever feel like I was going to die. It seemed impossible. I was a nurse, I was a Christian, I knew God had good plans for me. So even in that horrible, horrible moment I didn't think I'd actually die."

"What happened to him?"

"The police came. Between them and the security guards, they got him restrained. He's in jail, waiting for a court appearance. I don't think they're in any hurry to release him."

"Will you have to be there for that?"

"Maybe. One day. When I told the police I was coming here, they said I could do video testimony if necessary. We all hope he's going to plead guilty. Then it goes away."

"But not for you."

She exhaled and rested her ear against his shoulder. "I don't have the same nightmares as before. But it was tough, those first few weeks. The surgeons said it was a miracle, that if he'd pressed a millimeter harder I would've lost my voice, that if I hadn't grabbed my throat like that I probably would've died, because I lost so much blood." Another shaky breath escaped. "It was hard afterwards, to not think about that, that I could've easily died."

"God saved you."

"Yes."

Silence fell, the sound of leaves rustling in the light breeze. The stars continued with their gentle vigil.

"So that's why you wear scarves and turtlenecks."

She nodded. "I found that people don't really see me anymore, they just see this." She pointed to her throat. "They see the scar and think they know me."

"I see you," he said softly.

"What do you see?" Her words were barely breath.

"I see someone courageous and kind, cheeky and yet full of compassion. I see someone beautiful, inside and out."

"It's dark, huh?"

He smiled. "I see someone I'd really like to kiss again now."

"Really?"

"Really."

He took his time, exploring her mouth with his, celebrating life with her, yet knowing kissing wasn't really the answer, as he sensed she still had more to say.

She drew back, reluctantly it seemed, and smiled, before resting her head on his chest again. There was something so sweet about her, the way she treated him like her human-sized teddy bear, like she found comfort from being with him. As he did her.

"Thank you for sharing."

"Thank you for listening." Her hand slid up to touch his

stubbly chin. "You're a good listener, just like you said you were."

"I try."

A sound like amusement pushed from her, then she sighed again. "I don't mind if you want to tell the others. I feel bad I haven't told Ellie, but I couldn't find the right words, or the right time."

"It's not an easy conversation."

"No." A beat. "And I don't mind if you have any more questions. Better ask them now while I'm spilling my heart rather than wonder."

Okay then. "How long were you in hospital for?"

"A week or so, in surgery then ICU. Mum and Dad came out to see me. Mum ended up staying for weeks."

He nodded, remembering a request for prayers for the Franklin's daughter who had been involved in a terrible accident back home. Maybe they'd said incident. Regardless, the gossip had not relayed things accurately. As usual.

"It was so hard on them," she continued. "Mum already felt guilty for leaving me in Australia and coming here. I had insisted on staying, saying it was safer there. Ha. Look at me. Got it wrong. Again."

"You can't blame yourself."

"I get told that all the time, so you'd think I'd believe it. But if I hadn't left the desk like I'd been trained not to—"

"Then the druggie might've attacked the old man, who would've died," he said.

She stilled, then after a moment, pushed up from her nest next to his heart.

"What is it?"

"I never thought about it like that," she said. "You're right. The guy was so drugged out he was going to attack someone, and it probably would've been the old man who was so frail he might've died."

He caressed her cheek. "So you're actually a hero."

"Please."

But she was. And her self-deprecation only increased his admiration. "I'm so glad you're okay now."

"Well, not exactly okay, but not as bad as I could be. I just wish I'd done things differently, you know?"

Oh, he knew, all right. He wouldn't have bought Brutus. He wouldn't have let his mom work herself to exhaustion. He would've manned up enough to let his brothers know he needed their help. And he wouldn't have thought he knew so much when clearly he knew not much at all. But something he did know—at least, something he was learning—might encourage her.

"Lexi, you can't second-guess life. Stuff happens, people make choices that are dumb, that are hard to explain, that sometimes can't be understood. But God was with you, God still is with you, and He's got you here for a good reason. I know that."

"That's what I tell myself."

"And do you believe it?"

"Sometimes." She smiled and snuggled closer.

Her smile caught him in his chest. As tempting as it was to try to kiss away her pain, he knew a better remedy. His hand slid down her arm until he caught her hand and once more threaded her fingers with his own. "Can I pray with you?"

She nodded, and he took a moment to breathe and center his spinning thoughts.

"Lord God, thank you for keeping Lexi safe, for protecting her, and for protecting the other people in that horrible situation. Thank you that you have good plans for her, that she can trust you with all her days. Bring peace to her heart and mind, and help her know your love. In Jesus's name. Amen."

"Amen," she whispered, drawing close to lay her head on his chest again. She wrapped her arms around him, and he pressed another kiss to her brow, content in the moment to let the porch swing rock ever so gently, as they stayed in this private cocoon.

He closed his eyes, but his thoughts kept whirling, twirling with imagined images, shocking and gruesome, horror ebbing away as he prayed for himself as well. It was no wonder Lexi covered her throat through scarves and turtlenecks. Who wanted to relive that encounter on what would likely prove a daily basis?

Her gentle breathing suggested she'd fallen asleep, no doubt emotionally wrung out by her recount even more than he was from merely listening. And while he had no desire to sleep out here, he had zero desire to move her either.

The sound of a car engine pricked him to wakefulness and drew Fido's short, sharp bark, but it was only Denny and the boys returning from their trip to town, the rasp of the motor from the old ranch bus giving it away. He wondered if Lexi would waken, but the sounds of low voices, doors closing, showers humming, and the like didn't stir her. He was glad when the sounds ceased, and the peace of the night enveloped them again.

God was here. He could feel Him. Feel His presence around them. Feel His peace even now. God, who saved them. God, who healed. God, who restored, and made a way for hope to rise again.

He held her for a little longer, knowing he'd need to wake her soon, especially if they were to maintain that space of decorum between them that he'd tried to convince his brother of earlier. He'd be a hypocrite—and probably pretty damp—if he allowed her to sleep out here tonight.

He closed his eyes again, lifting prayers for her to know God's true peace deep within her heart and mind.

Lexi. Poor Lexi. His admiration of the woman in his arms had escalated even more.

She'd been so courageous, putting her life on the line for a stranger, even as it meant that due to her compassion she had nearly bled out and died.

Lexi, sweet-hearted Lexi. His sweetheart. The sensation deep within tightened in certainty. Earlier, he might've said he really liked her, but that was a lie.

This cowboy was full-blown in love.

CHAPTER FIFTEEN

"Good morning."

Jackson's deep voice drew heat to her cheeks, and awareness that they were the stars of the Reilly family morning show. Or at least so Ellie and Cooper seemed to think, having ceased their conversation the moment he stepped into the kitchen, their eyes glued to them.

"I think Lexi thinks it's a good morning now," Ellie said, earning a chuckle from Cooper.

Lexi glanced at Jackson, saw his grin, and her shoulders relaxed. "Hi."

"Hi." He leaned one hip against the kitchen counter, eyeing her like he was a starving man and she was a plate of toast and bacon and eggs. "Want some bacon?"

He glanced at the empty stove. "Uh, sure, if you're cooking."

Oh. Wait. She wasn't cooking breakfast. "Uh—"

"He gets bacon, and I only get cereal? Where's the justice?" Ellie complained as she gave Lexi a wink.

"Maybe he'd prefer a good morning kiss," Cooper said.

"I think he would," Jackson said.

Before she knew what he was about, he'd swooped in and pressed his mouth to hers, as if oblivious to the catcalls.

"All right!" Ellie wolf whistled. "Go the bro."

"Go the bro?" Cooper asked. "Did you seriously say that?"

"I'm just happy for him. It's about time, brother."

Lexi pushed her hand back against Jackson's chest. "Stop. I can't do this in front of your mother and siblings."

"Mom?" He turned. Sure enough, his mother was watching with a smile on her face. "Mom, it's great to see you up again."

"It was time. I've been in that bed too long."

Lexi's heart glowed as Jackson bent to give his mother a hug. Her time here had proved worthwhile.

"Wow, a night of miracles, huh? Mom getting better—"

"Oh, I—"

"Jackson got the girl."

"I—"

Ellie interrupted Lexi's protest. "No, seriously. I'm really happy for you two."

Lexi bit her lip. She'd need to explain that Mrs. Reilly getting up today did not mean she was completely better. Although, having lived with the family these past few weeks, she wondered if the diagnosis of early-onset dementia was premature. Perhaps it was more a case of complete physical and mental exhaustion. "We need to take it a day at a time."

Ellie glanced back at her mother, her face falling. "Oh."

"But it will help Mrs. Reilly to be out and about a little more," Lexi said.

"Jackson, what are you up to today?" Cooper asked. "Anything I need to know about? What's happening with the finances? Do you need my superior brainpower to help you?"

Lexi smiled and turned back to the washing up, listening as the siblings squabbled.

Jackson apparently did have some spreadsheets to show his brother. It wasn't long before the two of them moved to the office, and she heard Cooper's loud complaint about the state of the room.

"He's always been a little messy," Mrs. Reilly said.

"Jackson?" Lexi asked, pleased to see her making connections and engaging again.

"But he tries so hard."

"He's always wanted to help you, Mom," Ellie said.

Mrs. Reilly nodded, and Lexi wished he could see his mother's appreciation. Maybe she'd tell him later.

But the rest of his morning was taken up in other things—phone calls, cattle checks, fence work—so Lexi worked with Ellie and Mrs. Reilly to work out all the logistics involved in running a farm stay. As Dermott's wife had indicated, it wasn't enough to provide accommodation and a few experiences. They'd need to work on getting permits and approvals, as well as the website, social media, and other elements to help make this a viable business concern.

"I'd much rather just clean the bunkhouse than sort all this stuff out." Ellie closed the laptop. "It's doing my head in."

"I can help, if you like," Lexi said. "I've just got some laundry to deal with, then I can help."

"You don't have to do our laundry or our cleaning," Ellie said. "Isn't it time you had a day off?"

After last night's romance and unloading her burdens onto Jackson's broad shoulders, she felt like she'd already had ten weeks of holiday. Even if her sleep had been interrupted by Jackson waking her on the porch swing and helping her inside. How mortifying to have fallen asleep on his chest, then discovering she'd left a small patch of drool on his shirt. There was a reason she'd been keen to get the laundry done today. "I'm okay," she said. "Truly."

"Hmm. Must be love."

"Stop." Lexi flicked the dish towel at her, snapping it on her legs. Ellie squealed.

"Looks like someone's settled in," Cooper said from behind her.

"She deserved it." Lexi folded her arms.

"Ooh, yeah. Definitely like one of the family." But his curled mouth said he was teasing.

Her heart eased. "So what do you think of the proposal?"

"He proposed?" Ellie jumped up, clapping her hands.

"Please excuse her. My sister enjoys getting carried away, doesn't she?" Cooper said with an eye roll worthy of Ellie. "We were talking about the farm stay proposal, Big Ears." He poked Ellie in the side before switching his attention back to Lexi. "Which I think has potential, but obviously we can't rely on that right now."

"But it will help."

He nodded, chewing his lip as he considered her thoughtfully, then tilted his head to the office. She shrugged and followed, surprised Jackson wasn't there.

"He's out fixing fences," Cooper replied to her question. "But because he's there and not here, I figured it's safe to say this. He told me about your injury. I'm sorry."

"Oh." But somehow, the fact he knew didn't bother her like it once had. "It's okay."

"I think you're pretty remarkable to have gone through something like that, and still have a heart for others."

"Um, thanks?"

He grinned, and in that moment, she could see his likeness to Jackson. "Anyway, he's going to the bank tomorrow, and we need to somehow convince him that selling the land is not an option at all."

"I know he doesn't want to," she said. "I think he regards it as a last resort."

He nodded. "I have savings, and I know Mitchell is willing to put money in as well. Dermott would be doing the same if he hadn't already invested his in a new business. I guess what I'm trying to say is that it would be really good if you could convince him to accept our help."

"Me?"

"He listens to you, Lexi. He respects what you say. I think if you were to make the suggestion, he'd pay a lot more attention to you than he would his little brother."

She smiled. "You're only a few years younger, right?"

"You wouldn't know it by the way he speaks about me."

"What if he doesn't? Maybe you'd be better off going to the bank with him."

He sighed, and drew his hand through his hair, another move reminiscent of his brother. "I don't know if he'll listen."

"Maybe you should pray his heart is soft to your suggestion."

"So you're a believer as well."

"I don't think anyone could go through what I did without believing in God."

"But you believed before."

"Yes." She smiled. "I suppose it was inevitable with parents who run a Bible school. Why?" She suddenly was curious about his family. "Did your parents have faith?"

"We don't talk about my father, and it's obvious he didn't take his marriage vows seriously. Mom took us to church when we were younger, but she got busy and Sundays were often spent working."

"I bet that's easy when you live on a ranch, with so many calls on your time. But Jackson and Ellie prioritize church now. How about you?"

He shrugged. "I'll go. If I have to."

Looked like another prayer point stood before her now. "Well, it's a good thing our relationship with God doesn't depend on how often we go to church."

He nodded, looking away, and she followed his gaze around the room. "Jackson should clean this place up."

"I think the ranch has had its overwhelming moments," she said carefully.

"Looks like he's been overwhelmed for years," he muttered.

And maybe that was so. "But he's getting on top of things again."

"Yeah? How do you know?"

She couldn't explain how she knew. She just did. Maybe it was something to do with the light in his eyes and the way the heaviness of two weeks ago didn't seem to be there any longer. But whatever it was, she knew she'd do all she could to help him see his way forward. Maybe she'd even talk to him about using the bank of his brothers, instead of the one in Trinity Lakes.

———

JACKSON'S PHONE CRACKLED, the wayward breeze allowing the phone signal to connect for once. He dropped his gloves and pressed to answer, making a face as he recognized the name. "Jess."

"Have I caught you at a busy time?" the vet asked.

Any time was busy. He grasped the now-tightened fence post. "It's fine."

"Look, I won't keep you. I was just doing some more research about Brutus, and—"

"I don't want you to waste your time," he said. Or any more of his money. "I've made arrangements for him to be trucked away." Regret twisted. Poor Brutus. What a waste.

Silence met his ear. Then, "When?"

"Next Thursday."

She blew out a breath. "Look, I hope that'll give us enough time, but—"

"Enough time for what? I don't want any more testing."

"But—"

"Jess, I appreciate all you've done, but it's obvious. Brutus is a dud, not a stud. It doesn't matter what treatment we try, he's never going to perform, and—"

"I rechecked his breeding soundness exam results, and everything was fine."

"Everything looked fine, sure. But then he came here, and ever since then, nothing." Every time he had to explain was another stab to the heart. "I think it's time to let it go."

"I don't," she said bluntly. "I've had another idea and want to run one more test—"

"No."

A beat. "I'm sorry, Jackson. I just want to be sure. It would be awful to send a healthy bull to the slaughterhouse when it's simply an infection."

"An infection? Haven't we already tested for every disease?"

"Almost every disease."

He shook his head, clenching his jaw as he eyed the cows who Brutus should be breeding with. "No."

"Please? For Brutus's sake?"

He closed his eyes, scratching the scruff on his face. Why'd she have to guilt him with that? Why was he surrounded by women who pulled at his heartstrings? When had he gotten so soft? "Fine."

She exhaled. "Thanks. I'm going to use a sample we drew from my last visit. We should know the results in a day or so."

"He's still booked to leave for next Thursday."

"We'll have the results by then," she said. "And in the meantime, give the poor guy some time out in the fresh air. Who knows? If what I'm thinking is right, we might find the answer to our prayers."

Yeah.

The call ended, and he tried to refocus on the fencing, but the squally weather and Jess's last challenge unsettled him. Sure, God might answer some prayers, but there came a time when a man had to cut his losses and own his mistakes. Even if a miracle happened with Brutus, it didn't change the fact that Jackson had another meeting at the bank tomorrow. They needed finances now, rather than waiting on results that wouldn't be evident for another few months.

By the time he reached the ranch house, his mood matched the blustering winds. All he wanted to do was to find Lexi, spend the evening kissing, and forget all his worries. But she seemed a little distracted. When he finally got her alone on the sofa after dinner, instead of kissing, she wanted to talk.

She wrapped her hand around his, and despite her asking about his day, her brow held creases deeper than a newly plowed field.

"What is it?" he asked.

She shook her head, but he was tired of playing games. "Come on. You've always been straight with me. What's bothering you?"

"You have your next bank appointment tomorrow morning, don't you?"

He sighed. Why'd she have to kill the mood? "Yep."

She bit her lip, and his impatience surged.

"What is it, Lexi?"

"I wondered if you might consider another way forward."

"Like what?" he said. "Don't you think I've been through this enough already? What alternative is there but extending our bank loan?"

She swallowed, then looked at him. "Cooper said he had some savings, and that Mitchell—"

"No. Nope. I'm not accepting their charity."

"They're your brothers, Jackson. They want to help."

"Did Coop put you up to this?"

"He mentioned—"

"Great. So my brother goes to my girlfriend and tries to get her to twist my arm."

Her mouth fell open at his use of "girlfriend"—yeah, he was

as surprised as she to hear that word, but what else could they be after that kissing session the previous night?—then closed again. He knew he was being an idiot, but it didn't seem to stop the idiocy spilling from his mouth.

"I don't need to be told what to do."

"Your pride will be your downfall," she said, shifting away to face him more fully.

"So I get a bonus sermon as well. Thanks."

She shook her head. "No, I'm not going to fight with you."

"So don't fight. But I'm gonna find Coop and let him know exactly what I think."

And he did. And his plan to explain his point of view became a full-blown argument, where he questioned why Cooper insisted on sticking his nose into the ranch business, and Cooper countered by asking why Jackson had never shared the true state of the ranch finances.

"Because this is what I said I wanted to do," he said, conscious his voice was higher and louder than normal. "The ranch is who I am. Just like you're the tech whiz, and Mitchell is the hockey star, and Dermott is the gardening guru. I'm the ranch guy. I'm the one who knows what's going on here, not you. I'm the one who put my hand up to take this on. I'm responsible, not you. So quit putting your nose in where it's not wanted."

"Dude, I—"

"And you can quit telling my girlfriend you think I'm a failure."

Cooper held up his hands. "Whoa. I never said that."

Sure he hadn't.

Chest heaving with frustration, Jackson exited the room, only stopping briefly when Lexi called to him.

"What?" He tried to soften the irritation edging that word by gritting out a smile. "Sorry you had to hear that. Coop and I butt heads sometimes."

"He never said you were a failure," she said quietly, drawing closer.

Whatever. Cooper's actions going behind his back said exactly what he thought.

"You're not your job, Jackson." She clasped his fingers. "God doesn't love you any more or less because of what you do or how well you do it."

That might be true, but it didn't change how he felt about himself. "I don't know why you bother with me," he muttered.

"Jackson, I—"

He shrugged off her hand. "I can't do this, Lexi. I want—need —to be alone."

She stilled, and he brushed past her and moved out to the barn before he could see accusation in her eyes. There he found Brutus in his pen, looking as frustrated as Jackson felt.

He shoved fingers through his hair, grinding his teeth. Might as well add a dentist charge to their debts.

"Why can't anything go right?" His throat thickened, and he blinked at the burn in his eyes. He slumped against the wall, stretching out his legs as Brutus eyed him uncertainly.

"Sucks to be us, huh?"

He scrubbed a hand over his face. He didn't deserve Lexi. And she sure didn't deserve him. He wouldn't blame her for taking him at his word and leaving him.

But still, her challenge wove through his emotions. Sure, God might love him, but a man wanted—needed—to prove himself, didn't he? His brothers had all succeeded, climbing the professional ladder, making money, achieving. Which left him feeling left behind, the runt of the litter.

Panic rose, stifling the quieter voice begging him to pause, to be still. He pushed through, closing his eyes, straining to hear that whisper again. God loved him. God saw him. He didn't need to live with this constant fear.

Did he?

No.

He exhaled slowly. "God, help me to trust you. Show me what to do."

His eyelids lifted. In the dimness, he saw Brutus staring back at him.

A savage tug of pity for the bull pushed him to his feet, to slide open the big wooden doors, then move back to the pen and unlatch the gate.

"Come on, boy. You might as well enjoy your last week. Say hi to the girls one more time." Even if they had no wish to see him.

He slapped Brutus on the rump and steered him out to the pasture behind.

"Boss?" Denny. "What are you doing?"

"Giving Brutus a final chance at freedom."

Denny's whistle drifted softly on the evening air. "He hasn't had much luck, not since we had that hot spell of weather six weeks ago."

"It's been a warm one, that's for sure."

From in the distance he heard a cow's call, and the darkness pressing in reminded him he needed to return to prepare the financial statements for tomorrow's bank meeting. But before he did that, he had an apology to make.

Back in the house he found his sister and mom watching a movie. "Where's Lexi?"

"She got a phone call and said she needed to go."

"Go? Go where?"

Wait. She hadn't really thought he'd meant he wanted to be alone, had she? Panic rose, and he hurried down the hall, down to the room she'd claimed as her own. "Lexi?" He tapped on the door. "Lexi? It's Jackson. Hey, can we talk?"

He could hear movement inside, so she was in there. He pounded a little harder. "Lexi?"

Cooper paused at the end of the hall, his raised brows and

sardonic expression making it obvious what he thought about Jackson's oh-so-smooth ways.

Jackson ignored him. "Lexi, please, open the door."

Maybe she'd finally had enough. Even a saint would have run out of patience by now. But ignoring him like this didn't fit with her kind ways.

"Lexi!"

"Would you quit yelling?" Ellie shouted from the lounge. "We're watching a movie."

"She's in there, but she's not answering."

"Do you blame her?" Ellie said, her voice still way too loud. "You really think that's the way to make her care?"

His shoulders slumped, and he stepped away. Nope. It wasn't. He was so bad at this relationship stuff. Maybe he could make it up to her tomorrow.

———

"Mr. Reilly. How good to see you again. Here with your brother, I see."

"Millie." Good to know her eyes still worked. Maybe she'd see these projections and not weep. "Did you get the financials I emailed through last night?"

She nodded, her position across the bank desk suddenly feeling very far away. "Mr. Reilly—"

Honestly, did she get a power trip out of calling her old school friends like they were of his parents' generation?

"—I'm afraid these budgets and projections aren't going to meet our requirements. I'm sorry, but I must inform you that I am forced to start proceedings to call in our loans."

"No. You can't do that. It's Reilly land. It's ours. My great-grandfather settled it."

"Jackson—"

So now she wanted to be a human.

"I understand this is hard, but I'm not authorized to offer anything more."

Okay, so maybe she didn't. He stared at her, images of the ranch lifting and swirling through his mind like Dorothy's farm caught in a wicked witch-type twister. He could barely grasp what was being said. He leaned forward, elbows on knees, and did his best not to plunge his head into his hands. There was no reason to add to Millie's pity. *Lord, I'm sorry. I thought I could do this, but I can't. I really need Your help.*

Words rushed over and around him, but he could barely comprehend anything, as a stubborn thought teased him still. He opened his clenched hands, a silent submission to God's will.

"Could you please clarify exactly how much is due immediately?" Cooper asked.

Millie said the sum, the amount beyond Jackson's dreams. Maybe he could sell a kidney …

Cooper pulled out a checkbook and scribbled a sum. "Will that cover it?"

Jackson watched, feeling removed from reality, like watching a play from behind glass, as Millie glanced at the piece of paper, then glanced at him, then at Cooper. "That will stave off the most immediate debts, but there's still the longer-term loan for which we need to come to some kind of arrangement."

"How long until we need to do that?" Cooper asked.

She named a date four weeks from now, and the two of them talked around him some more, then he found himself shaking hands, still in a daze, struggling to comprehend what had just occurred.

"What just happened?" he asked once they got out onto the pavement. "You paid the debt. It wasn't your debt to pay."

"Actually, I think it was."

"What?"

Cooper motioned to the bench across the street, where Rhonda Ingalls, one of Trinity Lake's busiest busybodies, watched them with avid curiosity. "Hey, are you hungry? Let's go to Joe's."

Five minutes later, they were sitting in the diner's corner booth, having ordered two Trinity burgers, fries, and chocolate shakes like the overgrown boys they really were, the younger two Reilly brothers who'd rarely indulged in such treats growing up.

Their drinks arrived with Marlene's promise the food was on its way, which meant the fun and games of this conversation could begin.

"Are you going to explain what just happened in the bank?"

Coop loudly slurped his shake through a straw, drawing more than one eye in their direction, but the stress and weight of the past twenty-four hours meant Jackson barely raised an internal smile at his sophisticated-looking brother making such a sound. Ellie would've laughed and made a snide comment. He suspected Lexi would smile over it, too. Regret twisted anew. He hadn't seen her this morning, and he still owed her an apology. Which he'd offer as soon as he returned.

"Jackson, I'm sorry."

"Sorry? For what? Saving our bacon? Or for going behind my back?"

"Dude." Coop had clearly been in California too long. "You're gonna have to get over it."

He managed a tight smile for Marlene as she set their food in front of them then departed.

"I'm sorry you don't like this, and I'm sorry you've carried the burden of running the ranch for far too long. It wasn't your fault," Cooper said. "You weren't to blame for our father leaving and Mom not coping. And we were all content to leave you to run the ranch. And we shouldn't have, so yeah, I'm sorry."

Jackson stared at him, his food growing cold. "But I wanted to do this. I told you all that. You all agreed. I love the ranch."

"Yeah, you love the ranch, but it doesn't mean you got all the managerial skills that you need."

Wow. He picked up his burger and took a big bite, half hoping a bit of sauce would fly off and catch Coop in the eye. Mustard, maybe. Or hot chili sauce.

"Look, nobody likes being told they're not great at something. I get that," Coop said, as if his words didn't further twist the knife of Jackson's inadequacies.

"Just gonna point out that you're not so hot at saying encouraging things either." Jackson picked up three fries, shoved them in ketchup then straight into his mouth. "Are you seriously telling me I can't manage the ranch? What do you think we have Denny for?"

His brother eyed him calmly. "Denny is the foreman, not the ranch manager. And you need someone with a business head to help you." His brother bit into his burger, his eyes nearly rolling to the back of his head. "Oh man, I forgot how good these are."

Good thing he was enjoying it, because Jackson had lost his taste for food. "I see. So the someone with that business head is you?"

"Maybe?" Coop shrugged and took another bite of his burger. Nope. No splash back on the white business shirt to be seen. Pity. "But I'm not about to quit my career and live out here."

"Then what are you saying?" Jackson asked, pushing his plate away. He had no wish to be further indebted to his brother, especially now, when Cooper's every word made each bite taste like dust. "And where did all that money come from?"

Another shrug. "Like I said, I'm not about to quit my career. It pays well, which makes me wonder." Coop looked at Jackson. "When was the last time you paid yourself?"

"Paid myself?"

"I thought so," Cooper sighed. "Does Ellie know you don't

have an income? That you haven't had an income all these years?"

"No." Jackson picked up a fry, tossed it back again. It bounced off the plate and landed halfway across the table. "Call me stupid, but I thought that was how things went."

"I'm not gonna call you stupid, because I'm pretty sure you were just following in Granddad's and Mom's footsteps. And while Granddad had some great plans and did good things, we both know Mom struggled. How could she not, when she was raising five kids single-handed?"

Compassion for his mother curled through Jackson's stomach again.

"I think it's time that you spent more time with business-minded folks," Cooper said.

Like Liam Darcy. The thought rose to contact him again. Jackson took a sip of his shake instead.

"Speaking of, did I hear something about you talking to Liam Darcy about a solar farm?"

Was Coop a mind reader now? "I've emailed. He's been away. He hasn't got back to me."

"Try again." Coop picked up his burger again. "We should have them over, now Mom is doing better. I think it'd be good for Ellie to spend some time with Georgia."

"We?" Jackson arched a brow.

Coop raised one of his own. "You written that email yet?"

"Fine." Jackson got out his phone and typed while Coop finished his burger and gave a loud gulp.

"And you shouldn't blame Lexi for wanting to help. You know she cares about you, don't you?"

"Yeah, I do."

Coop eyed him, and Jackson pressed send on his message, the email flying through cyberspace with the familiar whoosh sound.

"Are you ready to leave?"

Knowing his brother lived in an income bracket way above Jackson meant he felt no remorse about letting him pick up the tab, offering Marlene a hefty tip for her trouble.

They were soon pulling into the drive, and the questions and explanations and apologies churned within. He couldn't wait to find Lexi and beg her forgiveness. He opened the door before Coop had unbuckled and was about to hurry up the steps when Denny called for him.

"Boss? There's something you've gotta see. Now!"

Jackson sighed, the weight of responsibility steering his feet around to the back yard. Fido's tail wagged ecstatically, and he gave her a scratch behind the ears as he drew near to the foreman. "What's happening?"

"Take a look." Denny pointed to the near pasture, where Brutus was—oh.

"Whoa."

"Exactly." Satisfaction lit Denny's voice.

"Good for Brutus."

"Mmm. I wonder if maybe he's finally recovered."

Judging from the bull's athleticism, it seemed so.

Something his Granddad had once said floated through his mind. Summer heat could render a bull temporarily infertile, and infertility could follow for sixty days after a fever.

He did the math. This wasn't quite sixty days. Maybe it was one of God's miracles?

Denny gave a raspy chuckle. "Looks like someone's finally figured how to get on with the ladies."

That made one of them. Which reminded him … "I need to get back to the house."

He clapped Denny on the shoulder, and hurried back up the hill, calling Jess Martin with the good news as he walked.

"Really? That's awesome. And what I hoped, too."

"So you think he's better?"

"I'll message you the results when they come through, but in looking through all the paperwork, I'm nearly one hundred percent positive he suffered some form of heat stress which affected things. But I'm pretty confident the results will show he's not firing blanks anymore."

Thank you, God. Now if only the bull's actions would result in calves one day …

He ended the call and slid open the glass door. "Lexi?"

"Is that you, Jackson?" Ellie called from the front of the house. He moved into the living room and found her sitting with his mom, looking at old photograph albums. "How'd it go?" Ellie asked.

"We're safe for another month."

She smiled. "That's good."

"Yeah. And it seems like Brutus is on the mend, too."

"That's awesome!"

He nodded, shoved his hands in his back pockets. "Hey, where's Lexi?"

The light in Ellie's face faded, her eyes sobering with sympathy. "I'm sorry. Didn't she tell you?"

"Tell me what?" His heart rattled, a cage of fear.

"She's gone."

CHAPTER SIXTEEN

I t was quite possible Lexi's brain was going to melt out of her ears. She studied the screen, stifling the inclination to scream, and rubbed her weary eyes. The dry-as-dust facts and online forms required greater patience than she had, but it was the only way to get this sorted and get out of here. She'd already spent far too long hiding, wishing she could be done without further explanations, without further tears. So when Ellie's comment yesterday had been followed by that phone call, she took it as a sign from God to get away, clear her head, and try to make sense of things, once and for all. She'd spent most of last night, headphones in, listening to music as she cleared the clutter from her room, hoping it would help bring a sense of order to her mind.

But trying to make sense of the present—let alone the future —was next to impossible when Jackson's words kept ricocheting around her heart. Did he really think her so judgmental that she was spouting sermons at him? She wasn't. Well, she hadn't tried to be. Maybe it was a natural side effect of living with Bible teachers for parents.

A knock preceded her mother opening the office door. "Honey? Are you almost done?"

"I'll be a little while longer. Sorry."

"Okay. Well, just so you know, we're starting our first session soon. If you finish before we're done, please come and say hello before you say goodbye. Oh, you know what I mean."

Lexi smiled. She knew exactly what her mother meant. Maybe it was part of the secret language all families shared. She'd seen the same earlier, when Ellie and her mom had been talking, sharing family anecdotes with Ellie starting stories her mother took over and finished. Ellie had insisted on caring for her mother so Lexi could be released today.

"Go. You deserve it. And I'll take great pleasure in letting my brother know you're not here," Ellie had said.

"Don't be mean to him."

"After he was mean to you? Don't spoil a sister's fun."

"He's been under pressure," Lexi had said.

"So have you. So go. Do what you need to do. And don't come back until you're ready."

Ellie had let Lexi use her car, and she'd had fun negotiating the roads, thankful to park with only the slightest scrape of the tire against the gutter. After collecting a coffee and some sweet treats from the bakery, she'd made her way to the college, where she'd counted on being able to use her mother's small office. More importantly, her computer.

But the past two hours had caused more strain in her brain than she remembered since sitting her nursing exams all those years ago. Surely things hadn't changed so much these days?

A ping alerted her to an email notification. She was required to attend the nearest State Police command for a fingerprint test. Her chest bumped. This was really going to happen.

She downed the last of the coffee, screwing up her nose at the bitter taste, and booked a time, then refocused on the online forms, making notes as she went. So much to do, but so much she wanted to do. Meant to do.

Finally she submitted the last email request, closed the laptop, and pushed away from the desk. Her head spun, the officialese having officially fried her brain cells. She needed a walk, a run, a swim, a ride, anything. She needed to breathe fresh air and make the most of the time she had here before duty called. And duty would call. She was sure.

Speaking of …

She flicked on her phone and saw eight missed calls. Three text messages. An email, and another message sent via social media. Tears blurred her eyes, but she didn't listen to or read a single word. She couldn't, not until she'd worked out the last bit of hurt from her heart.

Her phone emitted another buzz, and she stared at the screen, thumb hovering to answer. But she placed it down, taking temptation away, and then tossed the phone in her bag and went to find her mother.

The crowd of summer Bible school students looked all fresh-faced and excited. She noticed a few dropped-jaw gawks as she passed, but their opinions meant nothing. She'd spent long enough hiding, wondering what people might think of her, what people might say. So they'd never seen a scarred throat before. They had now. Big deal.

Her mother's voice drifted from the great room while Lexi took the second door that led into the back of the room. Her mother was out the front, outlining the program for the next two weeks, to excitement and nervous titters. Lexi smiled. It was hard to believe she had once been like that, all bright-eyed and bushy-tailed. Now she felt more bruised and wearied, but that was probably the effect of a sleepless night and questions, endless questions, that had plagued her.

Her mother's spiel soon ended. She beckoned for someone

else to take the stage, then joined Lexi in moving out of the room.

"So you're all done now?" she asked Lexi, brushing some of Lexi's hair from her brow in a tender way that reminded her of when Jackson had done the same.

She blinked away moisture and nodded. "Thanks so much for letting me use your room. It was good to be able to concentrate here."

"Any time, darling. You know you're always welcome. There's always room, no matter how many people are here."

"Thanks, Mum." She wrapped her mother in a hug, drawing in the scent of White Linen as she did so.

"How are things with Jackson?" her mother asked, not letting go.

Lexi exhaled. "I don't know. I'm trying to be sanguine, but he's got a lot on his plate, and I don't know if I'm something he wants to prioritize."

"Oh, I think he does," her mother murmured.

"How can you say that?" Lexi buried her face deeper in the soft folds of her mother's scarf, something she wore as a style statement, not because of any scars.

Her mother squeezed her gently, then released, putting her hands on Lexi's shoulders as she eyed her seriously. "Because I know that man cares about you."

She shook her head. "I don't know. I thought he did." His kisses certainly said so. "But I wonder if there will ever be a right time. He's so busy with a hundred other things."

"I think you'll find he cares."

"How?"

"Why don't you turn around and see?"

So she did, and her heart missed several beats. Jackson stood not six feet away, holding a bunch of red roses and a penitent expression.

HE TOOK a step forward then faltered, unable to read her eyes.

"What are you doing here?" she asked.

He wanted to ask the same but figured that would sound rude to her mom, who had spied him several minutes ago. "I thought you'd left."

"I did. To come here."

"Ellie said you'd gone. And I panicked and thought you'd left for Australia without saying goodbye, and I … I …" Oh, sheesh. He blinked back an unfamiliar burn.

Her face softened. "Jackson. Did you really think I would be so cruel?"

He shook his head. "That's the thing." His voice cracked. "I didn't think you could be. You've been so gracious and kind, and I know I don't deserve your friendship, let alone anything more. But I …" He glanced up. Mrs. Franklin had disappeared. "Can we go talk somewhere?"

"Sure."

He handed her the roses, and okay, maybe roses were a dumb idea, because now she had to use both arms to carry them when all he wanted was to hold her close. Or at least hold her hand. But he'd thought the gesture of flowers might seem romantic, might win her over. Or back. Or whatever. They moved outside to a stone path that led away from the imposing building, past some trees to a bench under a tree positioned to best capture the view of the lake. "Lexi, I—"

She stole the rest of his apology in her kiss, his expensive roses tipping to the ground as she wrapped her arms around his neck. He kissed her back fervently, ardently, reverently, his mind spinning, his heart twirling with gladness, like batons at a Fourth of July parade.

"I'm sorry," he breathed against her mouth, their foreheads touching. "I say dumb things sometimes."

"I do, too. I guess that makes us perfect then."

"Us." He kissed her again, long, deep, and thorough. "I like us."

Her smile sent shards of rainbow light through his chest. "I like you."

"Yeah? Well, I don't know if the roses were a clue, but I love you, Lexi Franklin, ma'am."

She laughed, and he took that as a good sign, gesturing for her to sit with him. She collected the roses and placed them beside her. "They're gorgeous. Thank you."

"It's hard to find nice roses that say I'm sorry and I love you."

She stroked a petal. "These work."

He grasped her hand. "Lexi, I want us to work. I know there are things I need to sort out, but I'm trying to trust God. I'm trying to trust others. It's hard to let go when I'm used to being in control. Or at least fooling myself into thinking I'm doing okay."

"I understand." Her voice, her eyes, held that dear sweetness he was coming to depend on.

"You really are the most understanding thing," he said, cupping her cheek.

"I know."

He grinned and swooped in to kiss her again. "So ... can I ask what you're doing here? All Ellie finally admitted was that she thought you might come here."

"I'm not leaving the country. Not yet, anyway. I was filling in my applications for transferring my nursing registration. It's not nearly as straightforward as I'd hoped, and every time I tried back at the ranch something—or someone—distracted me." She stroked his chest. "So I came here for some quiet, so I could finally get it done."

"Then we're okay?" he asked. "I mean, I know I don't deserve—"

"Would you stop saying that?"

"Yes, ma'am."

"And you can stop saying that, too."

"Yes, ma—Lexi."

Her grin poked out. "As far as I'm concerned, we're all good. But I won't think that you think that if you say that again. Okay?"

"Understood."

She exhaled. "Now, why don't you tell me how things went at the bank today?"

He explained about his brother, about his own lack of income, his lack of expertise. "I feel like such a fool, but I didn't know what I was doing. I just went in, boots and all, and tried to keep things running the way Mom and Granddad did."

She squeezed his hand. "I suspect ranching has changed a lot in the past fifty years."

"I think it's changed a lot in the past fifteen."

"So the immediate debts are paid. What about the mortgage?"

"Coop says he and Mitchell have a plan." Something Coop had referred to in the car on the way back to the ranch. He'd been too stunned to take in the details.

"Really? How do you feel about that?"

"Am I allowed to admit I feel a little relieved? I thought I had to carry it all, and carry it without complaining. Otherwise, it would seem I had failed, and just add greater pressure again."

"And your brothers didn't want to step on your toes?"

"That, plus I think they might've taken me for granted."

"What, family taking someone for granted?" Her friendly sarcasm faded. "It happens, but it's never a nice feeling."

No. But her laying her head on his shoulder was. "So apparently it's going to be a Reilly Brothers ranch, not just my thing."

"Hmm. I wonder what Ellie will say to Reilly Brothers."

He chuckled. "I'll let her take that up with the brothers."

"Good idea."

They sat there, watching the sunshine sparkles on the lake, arms around each other, as they took a moment to breathe, to relax, to inhale the summer scent of flowers, and the subtle scent of roses. He pressed a kiss to her hair. "So will you come home soon?"

"Home?"

He swallowed. "Back to the ranch." *Back to me.*

"Mmm."

He tugged her closer. "What kind of answer is 'mmm'?" He ducked his head and saw she was smiling.

His phone buzzed, and he drew it out to put it on silent, then saw who it was. "Uh, do you mind if I get this? It's Liam Darcy."

She straightened. "Then you need to answer." She gestured for him to hurry up, so he pressed answer.

"Liam?"

"Jackson, hey, how are you?"

"Uh, good. Look, sorry to bother you, but—"

"Hey, I just got back into coverage, and found a billion emails, including yours. Yes, I'm definitely interested in your land for expanding the solar farm."

Jackson closed his eyes. How he hated carving up his great-grandfather's land. Hated being the one who had failed. "Then I suppose we better talk price."

"Yeah." Liam mentioned a sum about a quarter of what Jackson had calculated as the asking price.

He frowned. "Are you serious?"

There was a beat. "We're talking the ten acres directly adjoining the solar farm, yes?"

"Yeah." He might not be much of a businessman, but he knew when he was being ripped off.

"Is that too low? We can go higher, if you think. But my business manager thought that was a fairly generous offer for an annual rent."

"Rent?"

"Yes. My understanding was that you Reillys didn't want to part with Reilly land, so I want to rent it. As part of the agreement, we'd cover all infrastructure and insurance and application fees. I'll have my lawyer send a copy to you, but if you have concerns then let me know. It's important to stay on good terms with our neighbors, right?"

He could barely breathe. "Uh, right."

"So you are okay? You let me know if you ever change your mind and want to sell."

"Yeah, that's not today."

Liam laughed. "We'll have to get together soon. You'll need to say hi to my fiancée."

"What?"

A friendly squabble came through the phone, then Liam's voice came again. "Sorry, gotta go. Apparently I wasn't supposed to tell anyone the good news."

"Congratulations. Tell Elissa I said hi."

"Will do. Thanks again. We'll be in touch soon."

The call ended, and Jackson rubbed a hand over his eyes. God was so good. So very, very good.

"Are you okay?"

The concern in Lexi's voice opened his eyes. "That was another answer to prayer."

"Another?"

He briefly explained about Brutus, which drew her laughter. "Well, good for him. Does this mean he's safe from being hamburger meat?"

"I'm praying so." Weight seemed to tumble off his shoulders. "And now with Liam wanting to rent the land—"

"Really? The Darcys want to rent your land?"

He nodded. "So we don't have to sell."

Beams of sunlight burst from her smile. "I'm so glad. God answers prayers, doesn't he?"

"He sure does." Like this woman, whose faith and confidence stirred his own. "Like you."

"Me?"

"You're the answer to a prayer I didn't know I'd prayed."

"Oh, you sweet man."

He swooped in for a celebratory kiss, which soon led to the kinds of kisses he didn't feel her parents would appreciate seeing. "You want to go soon?"

"I drove here, so I can meet you back at home."

"Home?"

She smiled, stroking a hand down his bristled cheek. "I love you, Jackson Reilly."

"You do?" he whispered, as his heart started thumping with the joy-filled refrain of a certain song by Keith Urban.

"I do." She pressed a kiss to his lips as if to seal her words. "So wherever you are, then that sounds like home to me."

THE END

Enjoyed this Trinity Lakes Romance?
Then check out the next in the series,
Where Our Hearts Lie by Jenny Glazebrook

A NOTE FROM THE AUTHOR

Thank you for reading *Love Somebody Like You,* the fifth book in the Trinity Lakes romance series. Several years ago I was lucky enough to visit some gorgeous towns like Walla Walla and Chelan in Washington state, and it was fun to work with other authors to create a fictional town based on these places. If you've enjoyed this book, please check out the pictures from my visit to Washington on my website at www.carolynmiller-author.com

Reviews help other readers find new-to-them authors, so if you can spare a moment to write a quick review at Goodreads / your place of purchase, I'd be very grateful.

Make sure you check out Ellie's story in *Tangled Up in Love.* And if you've enjoyed this taste of small town life then read the Muskoka Romance series, that starts with *Muskoka Shores.*

If you enjoy Christian contemporary romance you may want to check out the books in the Original Six hockey romance series, a sweet & swoony, slightly sporty Christian contemporary romance series.

The Breakup Project
Love on Ice
Checked Impressions
Hearts and Goals
Big Apple Atonement
Muskoka Blue

Romance and hockey fans may also want to read *Fire and Ice*, the first book in the new Northwest Ice series.

I'd love for you to check out my other books and to sign up for my newsletter at www.carolynmillerauthor.com where you can be the first to learn all my book and contest news, and discover more behind-the-book details and photos. Newsletter subscribers can also get an exclusive bonus book free, so grab your copy of *Originally Yours* by visiting www.carolynmiller author.com today.

ABOUT THE AUTHOR

Carolyn Miller lives in the beautiful Southern Highlands of New South Wales, Australia, with her husband and four children. A long-time lover of romance, especially that of Jane Austen, Georgette Heyer and LM Montgomery, Carolyn loves to write contemporary and historical romance that draws readers into fictional worlds that show the truth of God's grace in our lives.

To find out more about Carolyn's books, and to subscribe to her newsletter, please visit www.carolynmillerauthor.com

You can also connect with her at

<u>The Independence Islands series</u>
Restoring Fairhaven
Regaining Mercy
Reclaiming Hope
Rebuilding Hearts
Refining Josie

Historical:

<u>Regency Wallflowers</u>
Dusk's Darkest Shores
Midnight's Budding Morrow
Dawn's Untrodden Green

<u>Regency Brides: Legacy of Grace</u>
The Elusive Miss Ellison
The Captivating Lady Charlotte
The Dishonorable Miss DeLancey

<u>Regency Brides: Promise of Hope</u>
Winning Miss Winthrop
Miss Serena's Secret
The Making of Mrs Hale

<u>Regency Brides: Daughters of Aynsley</u>
A Hero for Miss Hatherleigh
Underestimating Miss Cecilia
Misleading Miss Verity

'Heaven and Nature Sing' from the Joy to the World Christmas
novella collection

'More than Gold' from

the Across the Shores novella collection

Where Our Hearts Lie - Jenny Glazebrook

No Matter How Far - Sara Beth Williams

Over the Rainbow - Meredith Resce

Tangled Up in Love - Carolyn Miller

In Truth and Love - Jenny Glazebrook